~BLUEBIRDS AMONG THE WHIRLWINDS~

To Priscilla —
A dear, delightful,
lovely lady! We
couldn't be happier
for Jason — he found
a prince — a princess?
Debbie

Deborah K. McDade

I am ever grateful to my husband, Steve who is God's treasure out of the ashes.

Publisher: CreateSpace Independent Publishing Platform
Date: September 20, 2013
ISBN-10: 1492776483
ISBN-13: 978-1492776482

May, 1928
Glendora, California

CHAPTER ONE

Hesitating for just a moment, Suzanne stood at the entrance to Olde Town Hall as the intensity within sent her senses reeling. She was keen on this new escapade; but never before had she experienced such chaotic activity. Her mother skillfully kept the cadence of her life restricted to well-structured segments of family, school functions, and a scrupulously appointed social calendar.

Deep inside herself, Suzanne wanted more! Her seventeen-year old spirit pulsated with yearnings and desires she did not understand. What she did understand was that if she lingered demurely in the drawing room for one more evening of tedious conversation, she would go mad. Feigning a headache, she asked to be excused, knowing that the family would expect her to retire for the night.

Later, when she'd slipped out through the French doors of her bedroom and stepped into the lush gardens, she actually did not have a plan, except to escape the house. However, as she had ambled along the meandering stone walks bordered by camellias, azaleas, and hibiscus and then passed through the rose garden, Suzanne realized that she was headed for the carriage house which was situated at the edge of the groves. The carriage house had recently been converted into a garage to hold the family's growing collection of automobiles.

Her pace had quickened at the thought that her brother, Edward, had been secretly teaching her how to drive the coupe. She was ready to venture forth and the coupe would take her anywhere she wanted to go. Still dressed in her smart dinner frock, she'd decided to try out the community dance advertised in *The Pathfinder,* her high school's newspaper. She was anxious to try out the Charleston and mingle with *those people* her mother called vulgar. Fortunately, driving came very naturally to her, and Olde Town Hall was not so very far away. Suzanne knew her dress was the latest style, but it was all white and she had never liked the way she looked without a trace of color to relieve the starkness. She felt her luxuriant auburn hair and light creamy complexion called for something more striking. Her mother, however, ascribed to Jane Austen's theory that "*A woman can never be too fine while she is all in white.*"

Tonight, however, Suzanne decided that nothing as mundane as a lack of colorful attire would get in the way of enjoying this amusement. Nothing could keep the sparkle out of her emerald green eyes, which people often called "gorgeous" or "fabulous" and thus they would be her colorful enhancement. Her small, well-formed mouth, curved into a smile as she slid behind wheel of the coupe, ready to strike out on her grand adventure into the unknown.

The only trouble Suzanne experienced on her surreptitious journey, was parking. There was so much coupe to fit into such a small space that she momentarily panicked, but then calmed herself as she carefully maneuvered the coupe just as Edward had taught her to do.

Parking without incident, she slipped a tiny mirror from her silver and black beaded reticule, using the full light of the moon to check her appearance before leaving the coupe. She looked a little flushed, but decided it gave her heart-shaped face a more interesting look.

Satisfied, she pulled her reticule together and with great anticipation, walked toward the hall. As Suzanne looked out over the crowd, she hoped there was another girl here that was her age with whom she could talk. In the 1920's, well bred society girls simply did not go out at night without an escort, especially to such places. Suzanne really did not know what to expect or how to proceed.

Pondering her predicament, she lingered nervously just inside the door.

About to plunge recklessly into the crowd, she stopped when she noticed that a man strode briskly toward her. Surprised, she dipped her head shyly. The society boys she knew would never approach so boldly; each acutely aware they had to be properly introduced first. This man-boy seemed to have no such constraints on his behavior. Indeed, he walked right up to her, flashed a mischievous grin and asked, "Do you have a comb? I seem to be missing mine."

Curiosity got the better of her and, Suzanne looked up to see a tall, well-dressed young man with brilliant black hair that fell in waves which curled at the ends as it fell over onto his forehead. The man's eyes, brilliant as blue sapphires, grew wide with amusement as she reached into her little beaded bag to retrieve a comb.

"Oh," he exclaimed grinning sheepishly, "that was just an excuse to talk. You are the prettiest girl in the room and I don't know your name."

Suzanne hesitated, but only for a moment. "My name is Suzanne." she said softly, "What is yours?"

"Jonathan," he said in a charming voice tinged with a slight southern drawl. "But my friends call me Jack."

As they glided out among the dancers, Suzanne felt her face blush crimson as her heart began to beat wildly. This was outside the bounds of all propriety; she was both thrilled and terrified at the same time. Nevertheless, instinctively she knew her life had acquired a new dimension and, she rather liked it.

CHAPTER TWO

Suzanne's world was changing like a kaleidoscope--moving and shifting in all directions. She thought about life and her future with an odd mixture of curiosity, sensibility, defiance, and nervousness.

Her grades were excellent, she enjoyed singing in the glee club, she was a top-notch tennis player, she loved her work on the school newspaper, and she dutifully attended all of the significant social events that took place in Glendora and Pasadena. By all outward appearances, Suzanne Antoinette Hughes was as prim and proper as was expected of society girls perched on the brink of womanhood in the year 1928.

Even so, on the third Saturday evening of each month she would feign a headache or say her stomach was upset or that she was feeling extremely tired and needed to retire for the night. As soon as she felt it safe, she would sneak out the French doors of her sitting room. Because the garage was located so far from the house, she was able to get to the coupe and drive to Olde Town Hall without being detected. Once there, she would scan the crowd for a tall, lanky frame. When Jonathan spotted her, he'd flash that sure lazy grin of his, sending little charges of electricity cascading throughout her entire being.

"You are the most beautiful girl in the room," Jonathan would whisper engagingly in her ear as they waltzed, danced the Jitterbug Jive or gyrated to the Fox Trot.

The clandestine outings to dance with Jonathan lasted all through the summer and on into the fall. Once in awhile, she would grow fearful of being caught, knowing her mother would never forgive her nor forget such an indiscretion. But, then she'd think about Jonathan and how stimulating he was; an exhilarating force pulled her towards him that she could not explain.

"He makes me feel as though I were dancing on clouds," Suzanne would think dreamily. Quite simply, she liked the way it felt and she did not plan to stop seeing him.

Life outside the bounds of her dull social sphere held lots of promise and Suzanne vowed she would find a way to experience it all. She was petite, charming, and beautiful; everyone she knew told her so. Secretly she acquired magazines that pictured sophisticated French fashions and printed the most entertaining, sometimes audacious stories. She was determined to be as modern as the glamorous women she looked at and read about in her cherished magazines.

"My hair needs to be bobbed." she thought determinedly. "Well," she'd surmise, "it will be as soon as I get up the courage to ask mother's permission.

Late into the night, Suzanne listened to the radio using a crystal set Edward had skillfully crafted for her. With the little crystals stuck in her ears, she would hum softly along with the latest jazz music, while her feet swished, "dancing" away under her great-grandmother's quilts. Her mother had forbidden such music in the house, saying it was vulgar. Suzanne thought it the berries; she was quite sure it kept her from being submerged in the mundane monotony of her family's very proper yet ever so dull life.

"I was born to be sophisticated, to travel, and to be a journalist. I am going to live out my destiny as a modern glamour girl--not as a wet blanket in some stuffy old house!" she would declare inwardly.

Suzanne was smart, her grades and achievements showed it. Going to college seemed to be the ticket to try out all the adventures that captivated her. Her family had plenty of money and getting into a nice woman's college should pose no problem for Suzanne. There were such schools in the East. Suzanne was ready to get a grip on where she was headed; ready to break out of the confines of her limited life in the little town of Glendora, California.

"Time to discuss the idea with my parents," she decided one lovely brisk afternoon late in the fall. The day held so much promise, she was sure that this was the perfect time to reveal her plans. "I will do it tonight right after dinner."

Her father, Charles Edward Hughes sat leisurely in the overstuffed "man" chair near the hearth while a fire crackled invitingly in the grate. Her mother, Grace sat stiffly on the pale green silk settee, her jaw squarely set. Suzanne stood as she passionately set forth her dreams. Glancing nervously at the appalled look on her mother's face and then at her shocked father, Suzanne realized the discussion was not going well. In distress, she redoubled her efforts to convince them.

"Certainly, we have enough money to send you to college," her father finally responded, then gently added, "but, what about getting ready for marriage? If anyone in the family goes to college, it will be your brother, Edward."

Grace brusquely asked, "What good would college do for you? You will be getting married soon, just like everyone else."

Stunned by this turn of events, without saying another word Suzanne left her parent's presence, feeling completely bewildered.

"Edward finished high school several years ago and he is not even interested in going to college," Suzanne stormed aloud once she reached the safety of her bedroom. "It is not fair of them to deny me this opportunity," she wailed as she threw herself on the bed.

As she lay sobbing, she thought of her mother going to business school in a day when most girls did not even finish high school.

"Don't they even care that I've always tried so hard. I was a straight "A" student, honored for many achievements at my high school graduation last spring. Why doesn't that count for something with them?" she stormed, thinking back over years past.

Grace Stuart Hughes was not an easy woman to please. Even after long years of trying, Suzanne had rarely succeeded in making her happy. Grace never hesitated to point out any small infraction of the rules while rarely complimenting any successes. Her father seemed helpless to stem Grace's maligning ways, though he always found ways to reassure Suzanne of his tender love.

As Suzanne fretted into the night, her resolve became unshakable. If her parents wanted her to get married so badly then she would do just that. She would find someone to marry right away and she would talk her husband into sending her to college. Surely, anyone who loved her would understand that she was destined to accomplish spectacular things in life and college was the way she could achieve those things. If her parents would not help fulfill her lovely dreams, she'd just have to find a husband who would.

Burying her head in the delicately monogrammed pillow, Suzanne thought of the possibilities. There was Tom. He was her closest male friend and long time neighbor. He was a great guy who often made her laugh. However, he was too steady and predictable for her; she wanted action. She needed someone who understood her, someone exciting, and definitely someone who recognized the fires she had blazing inside!

Jonathan, with his twinkling blue eyes, black curly hair, and charming smile was the one who had captured her imagination. Months of meeting in secret had turned into a crazy desire to be with him more than once a month at community dances.

Her quandary was that her parents knew nothing about her friendship with Jonathan. Besides that, she did not know anything about his family, knowing only that they did not move in the same social circles as her family did. Instinctively, she knew her mother would never approve of him or even like him.

Confused, she stopped to think about these troublesome issues, but rather quickly, decided to stop thinking about any such problems. She liked being with Jonathan, he was suave and interesting; and, he was so mature compared to the boys in her acquaintance.

"I just don't care what my mother thinks any more, I am grown up and ready to make my own decisions," she thought resolutely. Then glancing at the treasures scattered around her exquisitely appointed room, she cried out dramatically, "What good do all these mere things do me if I am not happy?"

"No matter what it takes," she determined, "I will find a way to get what I want out of life!"

December, 1928
Glendora, California

CHAPTER THREE

It was so very cold! Jonathan and Suzanne could see their breath as they walked toward the moss green home trimmed in sienna with sturdy cream-colored brick pillars defining the large terraced porch that Suzanne's grandfather had built for her parents. Feeling rather unsettled, Suzanne thought of the many times she had heard the story about the design of the house.

Her father and grandfather wanted to build a traditional Victorian Tudor mansion while her mother insisted on a Craftsman/Prairie style bungalow, which was the latest rage in home design when the house was built in the early 1900s. As usual, her mother won the argument. The architect designed an oversized Prairie style house to suit her mother. The odd thing was, Grace grumbled often and loudly about the layout of the house, complaining that it was too "restrictive" and "diminutive" for proper entertaining. Charles rarely responded. However, when his mother was visiting, she would stare coldly at Grace and say, "This design was your choice and yet, you constantly fuss about it!"

Grace would bristle and state forcefully, "It is the perfect design for a home surrounded by groves."

Charles' family of bankers, lawyers, and businessmen had never quite accepted the fact that Grace came from a family of "farmers." It did not seem to matter to the Hughes family that the Stuart family owned acres and acres of prime property filled with several hundred lemon and orange trees along with a large amount of walnut trees. The groves produced a steady, profitable income. For a wedding present, Grace's parents deeded the young couple several acres of property along with a portion of the grove business. Not to be outdone, Charles' parents had offered to build the couple a home at the property.

Nonetheless, Charles dutifully worked at his father's bank while an overseer ran the groves.

As Suzanne and Jonathan walked along the flagstone path bordered with a variety of colorful, well-tended flowers-- primroses, Iceland poppies, snapdragons, and delphiniums--and then up the terraced steps, Suzanne's thoughts nervously careened in all directions. On the other hand, Jonathan bounded up the brick steps ahead of her, passing between the square pillared columns, to open the door for Suzanne. As he did so, his entire being quivered with energy and excitement.

"I need to savor this moment along with him and stop worrying," Suzanne decided. "This is exactly why he is just the right man for me, he revels in life! And, I am going to enjoy it right along with him."

Grace, sparse in her affections and praise, was lavish when it came to entertainment and festivities. It was the 20th day of December and the Hughes' home was bountifully decorated for the season. The house was redolent with scents of pine, orange blossoms, cloves, cinnamon, and baking projects underway. Many expensively wrapped presents sat expertly placed under the handsomely adorned Christmas tree.

As was his custom, Charles was reading by the fire in the library, waiting for the maid to announce that dinner was served. Grace, dressed in a soft blue and ivory lace trimmed gown that made her face appear almost tender, sat writing at her desk. As usual, Edward was not present.

"I wonder when mother last paused to actually read a book. I can only imagine it was that French novel with a heroine named Antoinette," thought Suzanne irreverently.

As Suzanne brought Jonathan into the lavishly appointed room, her parents rose, their faces a stern blend of worry and inquisitiveness. Suzanne knew her disappearance today was not acceptable to them and so immediately she announced, "We have been married; please wish us well."

Grace promptly fainted. When she revived, a storm of hard biting questions ensued.

"How?"

"When?"

"Why? We do not even know his people!" Grace almost shrieked while clutching at the French bergère chair to keep from toppling over again.

"Oh Ma'am, I come from fine people," Jonathan interjected before Suzanne could answer the questions.

Grace looked up at Jonathan and frigidly exclaimed, "Is that so? We do not know them." Suzanne knew what she meant by that, but Jonathan did not.

"Well, ma'am, I am sure we could arrange for a meeting. I am Jonathan, but my friends call me Jack. Nice to meet you ma'am--sir," Jonathan said smiling politely as he bowed slightly to Grace and extended his hand to Charles.

Grace completely ignored Jonathan's gestures of good will as she turned to Suzanne. She had never seen her measured, reserved mother so apoplectic.

"Young lady, explain yourself!" Grace commanded.

Weary from all the years of submitting to her mother's furies, Suzanne suddenly lost her fear and retorted sharply, "You wanted me to get married and so I did . . . Today, at the County Courthouse in Los Angeles before a Justice of the Peace."

There she'd said it. She was glad, glad and happy to be free of her mother's control. For just a moment, Suzanne paused to look at her father's stricken face, feeling slightly sick at the thought of hurting her gentle patrician father.

Her defiance returned, however, when Grace summarily ordered, "Suzanne leave this house at once, you are no longer welcome here. I will send Edward with your things when you provide us with an address. Tonight, I no longer want to see your face nor do I want to see this Jonathan ever again."

In shock, Suzanne turned to leave.

Her father came to stand beside her, looking helpless and stricken. "Suzanne," he said tenderly taking her arm and reaching out as if to hug her, "I will always love you."

"Charles, that is enough," Grace commanded, then added severely, "It is this Jonathan she has chosen to love . . . instead of her family. Leave them to their own devices and let us go eat our dinner." Grace declared coldly as she went out into the entry hall and swept toward the formal dining room.

As usual, Charles followed submissively, while Jonathan and Suzanne walked hand in hand from the room; out into the dark chilly night.

CHAPTER FOUR

Jonathan's Model A bounced along the rutted road as they drove farther and farther out into the country, away from any surroundings familiar to Suzanne. The buttercup yellow frock and light wrap she'd selected so carefully this morning had been sufficient for a mild winter day in California, but the closer they got to the mountains, the more frigid the air in the drafty old roadster. Suzanne was cold from her legs, swathed in her best silk hose, to her delicate nose, which began to run most indelicately. She so hoped Jonathan did not see her wipe her nose with the hankie she'd slipped out of her little yellow clutch.

Suzanne knew what her mother would have said. "What on earth made you choose such a flimsy dress for a winter's outing? If you are cold, it serves you right!"

Even so, it was Jonathan's favorite dress. At the dance hall, Jonathan had declared that the combination of her yellow dress, her green eyes, and her auburn hair made him think of a daffodil filled meadow, alight with the setting sun. That comment had flung Suzanne's heart into a flutter of delight.

Her mother said her father had been poetic like that once.

Suzanne wondered at such a thought. She knew her father to be a gentle, sensitive man. However, a word like poetic did not seem to fit his personality; after all, he worked in a bank surrounded by stuffy old men and disgusting smelling money. Her parent's wedding picture showed her father looking ever so debonair with large dreamy eyes and a full sensuous mouth. Apparently, back then he had written eloquent poetry for her mother. He also played his guitar while singing of his love for her.

Not anymore, he was a serious man consumed with keeping his financial and social status intact.

Suzanne came back into the present and started to shiver which caught Jonathan's attention causing him to comment, "My lovely, you are cold! I am pushing this car to its limit hurrying to get you home to my mother. She'll certainly be more welcoming and let us stay with her for the night."

That thought made Suzanne shiver all the more. She did not know anything about Jonathan's family. When they had decided to elope, they never discussed anything as humdrum as where they would live. Suzanne just assumed her parents would provide a home for them as the grandparents had for Charles and Grace. Her thoughts had been solely on escaping her mother's watchful eye and sharp tongue.

Using the perfect foil of saying she was going to visit her best friend, Louise, Suzanne had slipped out of the house quite easily this morning.

Their trip to the courthouse had been filled with spine

tingling adventure. The return trip had been filled with silly songs and laughter. The car had not seemed the least bit uncomfortable then, but now Suzanne realized it was not at all like her father's Packard coupe. In fact, Jonathan's roadster was most uncomfortable.

Thinking about her father and the look of hurtful sorrow on his face earlier tonight made Suzanne aware she was miserable as well as cold. As she thought of the audacious thing she'd just done and her mother's final words, she began to feel rather frightened. Grace Hughes never retreated from a position and Suzanne knew she might not ever accept Jonathan into the family. It was quite possible that she would never again see her father or Edward or her cousins or grandparents.

Alarm seeped rapidly into Suzanne's soul. "What if . . ."

"We're almost there," Jonathan's voice rang out merrily interrupting her dismal reverie.

"No matter," she reasoned, "I love Jonathan and he loves me. He makes me laugh!" She was sure that they would always sing and dance, enjoying a most great and happy life together. She liked the way he was driving so fast, too fast, so that he could quickly make her comfortable again.

Suzanne placed her gloved hand on Jonathan's strong arm and serenely affirmed, "How wonderful, my dearest husband." At which they both hooted with laughter.

Jonathan deftly maneuvered the roadster around a corner and up a dirt driveway.

A sign at the bottom of the slight incline stated in faded, but very large red letters:

Maggie Mae's Boarding House
Come on in – Stay for Awhile

Although she knew a little about boarding houses from a novel she'd read once, Suzanne had never actually been inside one. She was not sure if she was excited or afraid. Her mother called people who lived in them "common" and Suzanne knew Grace carefully kept her away from anyone she considered to be such. Yet, she was just sure her mother was wrong, what could possibly be so different about such people?

Jonathan gallantly jumped out of his seat and ran around to open the door for her. Then, most unexpectedly, he swept her up in his arms and carried her up to the house. Giggling at the impromptu gesture, Suzanne did not see the woman standing on the porch until she yelled out shrilly, "Patrick, is that you. Where have you been?"

Hastily, Jonathan put Suzanne down and strode toward the woman.

"Ma," he said, his voice sounding strange, "I've brought someone home to meet you."

Suzanne was bewildered. "Who is Patrick?" she wondered.

"I'll explain later," Jonathan whispered in her ear as he came to stand beside her.

The woman he called Ma was rail thin, tall and rather attractive, but she looked quite haggard and worn out. As the three walked across the uneven wooden porch toward the red painted door, Suzanne looked up into the woman's eyes. They were unfriendly, hard, and calculating.

Suzanne's heart jumped and a shiver ran through her spirit. Her palms became clammy as she thought frantically, "Oh! What have I done?"

CHAPTER FIVE

The house was dimly lit and there was not more than a meager fire smoldering in the parlor. Suzanne continued to shiver as they crossed the cold room. She assumed the woman Jonathan had called "Ma" was the Maggie Mae of the boarding house sign. As they walked toward the lighted kitchen, Maggie Mae said tersely, "No boarders tonight, saw no reason to light the place up. Didn't want to use up the firewood neither."

They crossed through a large dining area filled with mismatched chairs and a table that looked as though it might have been lovely, at one time. Entering the kitchen ahead of Jonathan, Suzanne was startled by the shabby, sparsely furnished room. Relieved that Jonathan did not seem to notice her expression of distaste, Suzanne quickly gathered her emotions. Never had she seen a room so poorly kept--unwashed dishes were piled in the sink, the counter had crumbs and leftover food scattered about and the air smelled nauseatingly of stale food. "It will be a wonder if I can eat anything served out of this kitchen," Suzanne thought dismally. It seemed an unusual thought for such a time until she realized, they had not eaten since lunch time when they stopped at that tea room in Los Angeles. Jonathan wanted to celebrate their hasty wedding in style.

They'd happened upon a charming little, out of the way place that served tasty sandwiches and darling little desserts. It had all been grand, but now Suzanne found herself extremely hungry and rather tired.

"Patrick, what have you been up to?" Maggie Mae asked in a voice that brooked no evasive answers.

Suzanne still did not understand why she called him Patrick or why she did not ask them to sit down, leaving them standing, hats still on their heads.

"Sit down, Ma, and I'll tell you," Jonathan said in his most charming voice.

The three sat down at a table that was scratched, wobbly, and slightly soiled. Suzanne decided she would sit and keep a pleasant smile on her face while Jonathan informed his mother about their marriage.

"Ma, this is Suzanne. I met her at one of those community dances that you are always sending me off to, we've been seeing each other for several months now. We got married today, by a Justice of the Peace in Los Angeles. I hope you'll make her feel real welcome in our home." Jonathan said in a voice that sounded strained and rushed.

The look on Maggie Mae's face hardened; then her countenance changed noticeably as she assessed Suzanne with an encompassing look.

"So, you got yourself a society girl, huh, one of them prissy gals who won't know how to work. Well maybe her people will help out a poor widow woman like me," she whined, then determinedly added, "well that's what we've always wanted, isn't it, my Johnny boy?" with a sort of triumph ring in her voice.

Jonathan stood up abruptly and practically shouted, "No, Ma, it ain't that way at all! We love each other and we are going to have us a grand life and make lots of babies."

This statement made Suzanne blush. One did not say such things aloud in her home. In fact, Suzanne did not know anything about babies or how one was obtained. Besides, Jonathan was going to help her go to college first; after that she would think about babies. Right now, she wanted a comforting dinner and then a nice warm bath. She looked around the kitchen to see what preparations had been made for their dinner and was surprised nothing appeared to be in process.

Maggie Mae saw her looking and said harshly, "You lookin' for the maid? Ain't none in this house. We are it. How 'bout you take off that fancy sweater and your hat. Get yourself an apron and dig in. There are dishes and serving bowls in that cupboard over there. The pans are under the stove and . . . well, just look in the pantry and get something started. Patrick, come out in the parlor with me. I want to talk to you."

Suzanne was dumbfounded. She had no idea how to cook much of anything. She did not feel comfortable rummaging around in someone else's kitchen. Moreover, she was beginning to feel faint from the shock, emotions, and discomfort of the last few hours. So, she simply sat waiting for Jonathan and his mother to return.

When they did, Jonathan seemed distracted and almost fearful. She would ask him about it when they were alone. Right now, she assessed the situation and realized Maggie Mae thought she was helpless.

Suzanne felt a sudden fury rise in her spine which made her stand up and say, "Show me what you want done and I will do it."

Maggie Mae looked amused and started to speak.

"Ma," Jonathan interjected, "Suzanne is too tired to help out tonight. Tell me what room we are going to sleep in. I will take her up to get refreshed and then come help you myself."

"Take that room at the end of the upstairs hall. It's just right for newly married people. Get back here quick though, I need your help. It's late and I am hungry."

As Suzanne started to follow Jonathan out of the kitchen, Maggie Mae laughed loudly.

"Fooled ya, didn't I! There is plenty of cold stuff in the cellar and canned goods in the pantry. Let's just eat some of that tonight."

Jonathan shoved his black curls back up onto his head as he asked, "Ma, why do you do those things?"

Instead of answering, Maggie Mae stared at Suzanne with a piercing glare that Jonathan did not see as he walked away. He turned back to say tenderly, "Suzanne, honey, sit down and I will make you up a plate."

After which he turned and walked toward the cellar door, leaving Suzanne all alone with Maggie Mae in the dismal drafty kitchen.

CHAPTER SIX

It was hard for Suzanne to concentrate as they sat talking in the dreary bedroom Maggie Mae had deemed "just right." She was so very exhausted, the bed creaked every time they moved even slightly, and she was wearing a nightgown borrowed from Maggie Mae. Suzanne had never worn borrowed clothing before and she felt most uncomfortable.

"Jonathan, why did your mother call you Patrick?" Suzanne asked sleepily. "You said your friends call you Jack, but you never said anything about Patrick. It seemed so odd to hear her call you that . . . what did you talk about in the parlor while I sat in the kitchen?"

"My mother has some strange ideas sometimes," Jonathan replied.

"Like calling you Patrick when your name is Jonathan," Suzanne said suddenly feeling like giggling. Finally warm and not so hungry now, she was leaning against Jonathan as they spoke and it felt wonderful. Maybe things were not as bad as they first appeared; she liked this feeling of intimacy as they talked.

"My name is Jonathan Patrick. My father is English and my

mother is Irish. He wanted me named Jonathan, said it was a family name . . . she wanted me named Patrick, said it was her family's name. So they named me Jonathan Patrick and my mother always calls me Patrick."

"Your father has passed on, I am sorry."

"No, he is not dead. We left him on the farm in North Carolina because he became diseased and crippled. My mother didn't like it. Said she never liked being a farmer's wife anyhow. Now, she pretends she's a widow and tells everyone that she is, even though it's not true. When we moved to California, she legally changed our last name to her maiden name of Kelly . . . said she didn't want to think about the past any more. My mother acts like my father never existed. I really don't know what happened to my father. Actually, I haven't seen my father since I was nine years old and I miss him a great deal sometimes." Jonathan wistfully informed her.

"Oh, I see," replied Suzanne not really understanding such an extraordinarily cruel way of handling things. "How did you come to live in California?"

"My mother's brother, Gerard Kelly, came west long ago, said he'd always wanted to live in California, called it the 'golden land of opportunity.' He opened a grocery store in Pasadena which did very well. He kept asking my parents to come and join him, but my father always said no . . . said his roots went deep into North Carolina's soil, said it's where his feet felt most comfortable."

Suzanne almost started giggling again picturing someone

with roots growing out of his shoes and into the ground. She felt guilty thinking such silly thoughts when Jonathan was clearly sad about his father.

"So you came to California and . . ."

"My uncle bought this house for my mother . . . 'good investment!' he said, 'land will only get more valuable in this place, it'll be a boost to my financial status' . . . my uncle was sure of that."

"Why doesn't he help your mother keep the place up then?" Suzanne said without thinking, and then realized she had shamed Jonathan. "I am sorry, it just that . . ."

"I know, the place looks like hell, it's just the way it is," Jonathan replied defensively.

"Things will get better, you'll see," Suzanne soothingly told him. "What about the rest of your family? When will I meet your uncle? Does he have a wife? Children?"

"My uncle has a wife, but they aren't speaking to my mother right now . . . And, they have no children. I only have one brother, he's older than me, and he's in the Navy . . . stationed overseas right now. His given name is William Daniel. Everyone calls him Danny though. My mother's missed having his help since he left. She won't ever let me help her fix anything or do much work around here . . . tells me to 'just keep looking good and to work hard at my job.' She tells me that I am too clumsy, 'good only to be good lookin'," Jonathan sighed, trying to sport a crooked grin, yet looking rather dispirited.

"It is nice to learn more about your family. They are going to be my family too. I'm sorry about your uncle and aunt. Maybe they will patch things up with your mother soon. When will your brother be home again?"

"We don't know . . . he doesn't either. He'll just show up one day and say he's on leave for a few weeks. My mother tells everyone that he's her solid rock and I'm her pretty boy. I don't really like her saying that, it gives me the shivers sometimes . . . like I'm not a real man or something. We need to get our own place where I can take care of you and show the world I am a man!" Jonathan spoke emphatically as he hunched his shoulders forward as if to shake off any ill feelings of malcontent.

Singing softy in Suzanne's ear, Jonathan told her how much he loved her and wanted to kiss her and hold her forever and ever. Then finally he crooned, "Go to sleep my love, you've had a very long day."

Sleep sounded marvelous to Suzanne who was barely keeping her eyes open. She did wonder about those marital duties her mother was always moaning about. "Oh well, that is for exploring tomorrow," she thought as she dropped off to sleep.

Hours after, Suzanne woke for a moment and realized that Jonathan had left the bed. She wondered, but quickly returned to her dreams.

In the night she was sure that she heard footsteps and doors slamming.

"How unusual," she contemplated later, and then she

shrugged, feeling pretty certain she had only imagined those things because after all, she'd been sleeping in a strange new place.

CHAPTER SEVEN

The days stretched before her like a wild canyon which sometimes appeared to be filled with surprises of delight while other times with strange forebodings.

Jonathan had inducted her into the ways of "martial duties." She found the whole notion of "them" rather pleasant and wondered why her mother called them duties. Jonathan could be ever so tender, though sometimes impatient with her lack of understanding. She was working hard at learning.

Suzanne waited all day for those hours they spent together in the creaky old bed. She enjoyed the intimacy of being near him, the pleasantness of talking into the night, the warmth of sharing thoughts as they never had prior to marrying. No one had ever listened so very carefully before as she expressed her feelings, not even her best friend, Louise.

"Honey, you are the prettiest thing I've ever seen. You make my head spin round and round. My life has become like heaven with you!" Jonathan would tell her as he ran his thumb along the curve of her cheek, tangling his hands in her hair, and pulling her close for a playful kiss that soon turned passionate.

She was mesmerized by those euphoric joys, yet was waiting for the right time to talk with Jonathan about college and finding their own place to live. In the secret places of her soul, she imagined her mother relenting so she could move back with Jonathan to live among the lovely gardens and fragrant groves again. Surely once mother came to really know and understand Jonathan, she would reconsider. It seemed he charmed everyone else. However, when she faced the reality of her mother's unrelenting stubbornness, Suzanne could quickly grow despondent

Life in the sprawling old house with Maggie Mae's harsh ways, in a household with all sorts of strange oddities, was hard to bear. Christmas Day had come and gone with no gaiety at all. The long winter days droned on, with little to occupy her mind and time. Although, it was a relief to be free of her mother's tyrannies, Suzanne missed her father terribly. Of course, everything about the luxuries she had so casually embraced now appeared vastly more precious.

When Edward brought some of her things over to the house, most of her books had been included in the delivery. The books became her solace. Stretched out on the window seat, they appeared as friends ready to bear her away to soothing places of content. Jonathan even brought home a copy of F. Scott Fitzgerald's *Great Gatsby* after she told him her mother had forbidden her to read it.

Suzanne carefully placed her many treasures in such a way that they made her feel surrounded by their comforting presence and, it had been a great relief to begin wearing her own clothes once more, though Edward had brought only a portion of her extensive wardrobe. Suzanne was certain it was her mother who had decided that she would need only the most basic necessities for her new life. And it was true, Suzanne spent much of her day curled up in the shabby wingback chair, reading and dreaming; rarely did she leave the house while Jonathan was at work.

Sometimes she thought of home and her old life. It seemed to be slipping farther and farther away. She thought often of her father and wished for a way to see him. Other times she would ponder the look of incredulous horror mixed with curiosity on Edward's face when he drove out to the boarding house to deliver her things.

"What kind of place is this that you are living in, Sis," he had queried while peering around at the shabby porch furniture and peeling paint. She had not let him come into the house, she was too uncertain about Maggie Mae.

As she pondered, Suzanne would become confused about the whole operation of a boarding house. It was her understanding that boarders usually lived in them, at least for a certain length of time, as though they were living in a home. Around here, there never seemed to be anyone who actually stayed, just a few men coming and going at a hurried pace, usually late in the evening. Then there were those strange sounds that woke her in the night: doors opening and closing, scurrying footsteps, groans and strange creaking noises.

"It must be my imagination," she would reason the next morning.

Strangest of all, was that door at the other end of the hallway that Maggie Mae had forbidden her to enter, ever!

The one time she'd asked Jonathan about it, his voice was emphatic as he said harshly, "Just do what my mother says, Suzanne, it is best that way!"

His brusqueness wounded her. Suzanne complied as she was terrified of angering Maggie Mae. Nevertheless, she still wondered.

Then there was Maggie Mae's way of living. It stunned Suzanne. She had been raised by a brisk woman who used her days industriously and expected her family to do the same. Grace Hughes made certain everyone in the household was up and busy early in the day. As such, the Hughes home always ran in perfect order whereas Maggie Mae's house was generally in dreadful disarray and never really clean. For Suzanne, the oddest part of it all was that she never even appeared to notice.

Social events, familial duties, civic responsibilities, and proper manners governed the lives of Charles and Grace Hughes. Conversely, Maggie Mae did not leave the house much nor did she appear to have any friends. Obligations appeared to enter the mind of Maggie Mae Kelly rarely, save for making a meal each evening--one that generally left a lot to be desired. Maggie Mae's manners, her lifestyle, and even her way of speaking to everyone, from tradesmen to her son, would quickly be labeled vulgar by the people Suzanne had always known. She simply could not comprehend Maggie Mae's unseemly behavior.

Most days, after grabbing just a sketchy breakfast, Jonathan left early to work at Uncle Gerard's grocery store while Maggie Mae did not appear until sometime in the mid-afternoon. When she did, Suzanne made herself scarce as Maggie Mae would stagger into the "formal parlor" looking bleary eyed and acting very grumpy. She was usually still wearing her dressing gown, which unlike anything else about her life, was fancy and luxurious.

Suzanne soon came to understand that when dinnertime drew near, Maggie Mae expected her to be in the kitchen, ready to help. She was learning fast. Suzanne never again wanted to feel inept in the presence of that woman, thus she always acted confident and sure of herself.

Almost every evening Maggie Mae would state tonelessly, "Gotta always keep the men folk satisfied. Time to put supper on the table for Patrick." It was still difficult for Suzanne to remember that she actually was talking about Jonathan.

Sunday mornings, Jonathan and Suzanne usually packed a picnic lunch, along with a jug of homemade wine, to go exploring in the Model A. Sometimes they drove all over the verdant countryside, seeking for out of the way places that Suzanne had never visited. Jonathan liked to fish and he taught Suzanne how. Often, they went for long walks, hand in hand, through well worn paths in the foothills of the San Gabriel Mountains. They would sing, they would laugh, and they would lie side by side among the wild lavender and pungent sage as they would dream.

Every month they attended the community dance. Suzanne reveled in the noisy crowded atmosphere after so many days of solitude, finding everything about it intoxicating. She always wore one of her nicest frocks as she certainly did not need them now for any social events. Jonathan's good looks and charm seemed to draw them into a circle of exhilarating camaraderie with the other dancers.

Jonathan and Suzanne became so expert at the Lindy Hop that some suggested they enter dance contests or participate in a dance marathon. Jonathan would usually partake of one or two beers, which although prohibited, always seemed available from a hidden back room. As they drove home, he'd sing lustily. One of his favorites was a song recorded by Aileen Stanley titled *Everybody Loves My Baby (But My Baby Don't Love Nobody But Me)*.

Occasionally, they went to the cinema. Suzanne thought Clara Bow so beautiful and Mary Pickford so talented. She loved to see the costumes and lavish sets in the movies. Jonathan said he liked to gaze in wonder at Marion Davies. When they returned home, he would strut around imitating Douglas Fairbanks and his swashbuckling antics, making them both laugh uproariously.

These were the best of days, helping Suzanne forget all else.

Suzanne was certain they would move soon. Jonathan liked to sing about skies of blue and when they had their own place, she would find a way to reconnect with her family and her old life. Better days were out there for them, somewhere; she was sure of it!

CHAPTER EIGHT

The indigo of dawn was dispelling as the mountains turned from mulberry to amethyst and then to soft peach as the sun began its ascent for the day. Gossamer wisps swirled in exquisite cloud formations around the peaks. The air was crisp and still. Suzanne lay quietly beside Jonathan reveling in the beauty. What enchantment to watch the scene unfold within the framework of the big bay window. How it refreshed her!

The late April wildflowers carpeted the fields behind the house and Suzanne intended to spend another morning walking among them, contemplating. It was time to broach the subject of college with Jonathan. She loved the long evenings spent with him this past winter--sometimes reading together, other times listening to the latest tunes, and often enjoying amorous interludes. The sensation of floating, taking no action whatsoever regarding their future, allowing the tides of time to ebb away, had been most enjoyable. But enough of this languor--time to move forward!

Suzanne felt she had waited patiently for Jonathan to secure a house to call their own. She had endured Maggie Mae's disparaging remarks. She had slowly adjusted to the disorder and lack of refinement. Now she was ready to create their own separate life, away from this eerie old house, far from Maggie Mae's appalling ways. Truthfully, she hoped they never had to return to this creepy place. Suzanne was certain Jonathan would understand the necessity of pursuing her college education. They would move to the east where she could enroll in college to become a journalist and the person she intended to be. It was time to start the process.

"No matter if anyone understands or agrees, it is what I want to do," mused Suzanne, looking distractedly around the bedroom.

What a difference a bit of rearranging, a thorough cleaning and a few pleasant additions made in this room. On their Sunday morning adventures, they had picked up bits of unusual wood and rock formations that Suzanne cleverly arranged with her own treasures to infuse a bit of whimsy into the room. Pressed wild flowers added some color to the dark, drab decor. Lace curtains, replacing the heavy drapes at the east window, allowed more light into the room.

Suzanne thought back to several weeks ago when Maggie Mae had unexpectedly announced, "Tomorrow, Suzanne, we are driving to Pasadena with Patrick and then taking the streetcar to Los Angeles for some shopping. We will find a place to eat lunch on Broadway and spend the whole day in the city. "

As usual, Suzanne thought, "Who's Patrick?" But, then she quickly remembered Maggie Mae's strange penchant for calling Jonathan by his middle name. Although uncertain about spending an entire day with Maggie Mae, the thought of strolling among the shops and being in the crowded city again was irresistible to Suzanne.

Upon seeing her delight, Jonathan said sternly, yet flashing his most charming grin, "Well, Ma, if she's going to have a good time she'll need some money. I'll give her some and you; well you should give her some too. Not only that, you must also let her choose some shops she'd like to visit."

As the day of shopping had unfolded, Suzanne was surprised at Maggie Mae's relaxed, happy demeanor. It did not seem possible that she could be such. Suzanne purchased the lace curtains she wanted for their bedroom window and a book about wildflowers at Woolworth's Five and Dime as well as silk stockings along with an enchanting pair of new shoes at Bullock's Department Store.

They had lunch at Boos Brother's cafeteria. Although, it was not exactly a charming little café such as Suzanne would have chosen, it was tasty. Afterward, they bought a new hat for Jonathan at the Desmond's store. Maggie Mae seemed rather pleased about the purchase. At the end of the day, they bought a bag of sarsaparilla drops to take home. Altogether, it had been quite a grand day.

Gradually, however, Maggie Mae returned to her former acerbic, grim-faced self. Suzanne's dissatisfaction with their living arrangements grew ever more powerful. Her discovery of the fields of wildflowers behind the house helped create a tolerable diversion and she spent several spring mornings rejuvenating amidst their transient beauty.

Today, she would take a long walk and garner her courage in preparation for a serious talk with Jonathan.

"It has been a lovely few months together, hasn't it Jonathan," Suzanne commented softly as they settled into their bedroom for the evening. "Now, I am ready to talk more seriously about our future."

Jonathan grinned, "Suits me mighty fine."

"I never told you about the terrible scene with my parents when I talked to them about going to college last fall. I want to be a journalist. I want to move to the east so I can enroll in a woman's college. You could get a job in a grocery store somewhere back there. We could make a wonderful life on our own together, keeping each other happy." Suzanne gushed with passionate certainty.

"That's the most cockeyed scheme I've ever heard about," Jonathan said derisively. "What does a woman need with a college education? Women are intended to make babies, lots of them, and take care of the house. What do you mean you want to be a journalist? Your job is with me, being my wife."

Suzanne felt a chill of resentment run through her at that remark.

"What makes you think you can talk to me like that," she fired back. "I want more for my life. If that had been what I was looking for, I would have married someone with more prospects.

Remember, you said we could do anything we wanted to in our lives together and this is what I want."

Jonathan's voice was cold as he replied, "Well, I'm the one you married, ain't I? My prospects seemed to suit you just fine in December. No wife of mine is going to college or becoming a journalist. You better put that thought out of your head. What college would take a married woman anyway, have you lost your mind?"

It had never occurred to Suzanne that being a married woman would prevent her from attending college. Of course, that would most likely be the case. Why hadn't she realized it sooner? Why hadn't she thought everything through before she got herself into this situation? Now she was stuck--stuck in this shabby house, stuck with people who did not speak or act properly, stuck with a man who was not trying to understand her dreams, a man who brought her to live here with his incomprehensible mother. She was stuck, stuck, stuck. Fury engulfed her spirit.

"I hate living in this house. If you are so set on me taking care of a home, then why have you not provided one for us? You've had more than sufficient time to do so." Suzanne articulated sarcastically as she prepared for bed. "Good night, Jonathan."

When he stormed out, slamming the door behind him, Suzanne told herself that she did not care. Nevertheless, she spent the night in sleeplessness, tossing about, reliving the conversation, and regretting her tempestuous remarks.

And, Jonathan did not return to their bedroom that night nor did he appear the next morning.

CHAPTER NINE

Suzanne sat down hard in the old oak chair. She could feel her mind spinning as she tried to assimilate the conversation she had inadvertently overheard this morning. In her eighteen years of living, she had never encountered such particulars and therefore badly needed help to sort things out.

"I could talk to Louise," she thought, but quickly discarded the notion. "No, though Louise has been such a good friend in the past, she would not really be of any help to me in this situation."

"I'll confront Jonathan," she thought and again discarded the notion. She had not seen Jonathan since their fight last night. "Besides, he'd likely act as though I was behaving like an ill-tempered child," Suzanne reasoned.

"Who can help me know what to do?" she mused. "My mother will just flat out state that she told me so."

As though the sun had just escaped the clouds, Suzanne suddenly knew what she would do--her father was the one. "He will be gentle and comforting, even if it will be hard to truly capture his attention," she thought out loud, then jumped wondering if anyone had heard her.

Suzanne walked out the bedroom door and peeking out she saw Maggie Mae standing just inside the last doorway, looking at her with dark suspicion and something akin to hatred in her eyes.

"I need to pick up some things in town for Jonathan. I'll be back after awhile."

Maggie Mae replied coldly, "I don't care where you go, just don't be late for supper, you know how your husband hates waiting for his food. Lord knows why he even bothers with you at all. You sure don't seem good for much to me." Tempted to make a saucy reply, Suzanne held her tongue because she wanted to get out of the house as quickly as possible.

Although it was a long walk to the stop where she could catch a bus that would take her to where she could catch a streetcar into town, Suzanne just wanted to get away from that ghastly place. Her frustrations, fears, and confusion caused her to walk very rapidly.

As she approached her father's bank, Suzanne worked at composing herself. It would never do to appear disheveled, Suzanne was certain that somehow her mother would hear about it and would never stop reminding Suzanne that she had appeared in public looking less than perfectly assembled.

"I need to see Father right away," she told one of the clerks, speaking calmly.

"Yes, Miss Suzanne," he replied, "I think your father is in his office right now."

"Oh, my darling girl, come with me," her father whispered

as he held open the elaborately scrolled walnut door that led to the bank's inner sanctum.

After hugging Suzanne long and hard, he pulled out one of the finely tooled leather chairs for her and then sat down in another beside her.

"It is so wonderful to see you! What brings you down to the bank? Fortunately, I do not have a meeting for another half an hour or so. Tell me--what is on your mind today, Suzie girl? You look pensive and rather shook up. But, oh my goodness, it is grand to see you again! I have missed you so."

Her father's tenderness and use of her childhood nickname soothed Suzanne's wounded spirit and to her embarrassment, the tears would not stay put.

"Oh, my dear, dear father," she gasped and she held out her hand to be grasped firmly in his strong one, "I am so happy to see you too!"

She stopped for a moment, almost unable to go on. Then struggling with her emotions, and trying to sound mature, she spilled out the story. "Father, I came to see you because I have learned the most appalling thing about Jonathan's mother today. I overheard her berating one of the tradesman at the back gate. He'd had enough of it so he yelled at her, 'You're just a worn out old whore, everyone in town knows it, don't put on your airs with me, shouting at me so the whole street can hear you. You can't hide what goes on around here, you're a madam, a crazy old madam runnin' a house of ill repute, sure as my name is Sam.'"

The room was painfully quiet as her father absorbed this information. He did not look at Suzanne nor did he look surprised, making Suzanne wonder what he already knew.

"If she knew, mother would gloat gleefully at how accurate she was about Jonathan's family, but that is not the point right now. I am married to Jonathan and I live in that house, with her. What did that man mean exactly by house of ill-repute, it does not sound very good, though I think that I know what whore means, maybe. I am just not sure . . ." Suzanne shivered as she added rapidly. "Daddy, help me!"

Her father rose and fiercely scooped her into his arms.

"Oh, precious Suzie girl, I wish it were not so. I am involved in so much that goes on in this town that I know too much about its inhabitants not to hear the scuttlebutt and gossip. Yes, I have heard rumors about Maggie Mae Kelly's activities. I have never told your mother . . . though I've been most concerned . . . and not known quite what to do about it all. However, what's done is done! Well, though maybe we can find a legal way to get you out of this. As far as I am concerned, you are most welcome to come back home. Your mother, though, is a different story."

Weeping, Suzanne replied, "Yes, she made her feelings perfectly clear last Christmas when she ordered us out of the house. Oh, father, thank you for still loving me so."

"I do, Suzie girl, and I hate seeing you torn up like this, it makes me furious at Jonathan for doing this to you. I feel like I could . . ."

"Oh, father, no, I love him, my time with Jonathan has been really . . . until recently, it's just that . . ."

"Has he hurt you?"

"No, we had a terrible fight last night . . . about me going to college and us moving out of that house and I said some things I shouldn't have said and . . ."

"Come home, come back to us. I will help you. I will deal with your mother. I can make certain Jonathan will not come near you, we will work this thing out together."

Suzanne's pride swelled and she steeled her heart stubbornly, "No, Daddy, you have helped me see what I need to do, by just making those statements. I married Jonathan and we need to work it out. As mother would say, I have made my bed, now I must lie in it. That always struck me as such a strange thing to say, but I guess I am finding out about it now. I cannot simply waltz back home, take my place at your table, and pretend I am still a little girl. Thank you, father, thank you for taking time to see me. I do hope I can get to visit with you again soon. Good-bye. Maybe I will come to the bank another time to see you. Good-bye. I do love you."

As she trudged back to the streetcar stop, Suzanne could not stop thinking about how stricken her father had looked as she left him. It cut clear to her heart to see him that way. She was also still pondering just what that man Sam meant by a "house of ill-repute." It most likely had something to do with those men that came to the house late in the evening and that door at the end of the hallway, and those noises in the night, Suzanne shivered again. She was not so sure that she wanted to know.

"Jonathan will just have to tell me," she decided. "No matter, we will have to work this out, he's my husband. I will have to make him realize tonight that we must move to our own place now, not later! He must simply find a way. I will tell him--it is either that or I am leaving. That is what I will do." Suzanne resolved, determined to be strong. She felt more courageous now that she knew her father would let her come back home.

"I will go back only if I must," she whispered determinedly as she walked across the shabby porch and pushed open the red painted door.

CHAPTER TEN

It was unnaturally quiet as they sat eating their dinner together. No matter how often Maggie Mae and Jonathan called this meal "supper," for Suzanne it would always be dinnertime. Jonathan seemed distant and morose. He had come in from work, simply washed up, and then sat down to wait. Suzanne felt exhausted from her long walk and turbulent emotions. Even Maggie Mae was subdued tonight, appearing altogether haggard.

Even though she dreaded the encounter, Suzanne was anxious for the meal to pass so she could ask Jonathan to join her in their bedroom for a much needed talk. She was not even certain he would agree to it, as they had not spoken one word to each other since last night.

"Jonathan, let's go up to our room right now and try to work things out," Suzanne whispered softly in his ear as Maggie Mae left the room, glowering at them both as usual.

He stood still for almost a full minute, and Suzanne feared he was going to say no. However, he surprised her by saying, "Yeah, let's go, it's been a terrible day for me."

While they walked up the stairs, side by side, Suzanne

pondered just what to say first. She need not have worried, the minute the door was shut, Jonathan swept her up in his arms in the fiercest of hugs while talking into her hair, "Oh, my sweet darling, I wasn't sure you'd even be here when I got home tonight. It was a horrible day. You are my wife . . . you are the most beautiful girl I ever danced with and it is my responsibility to find us a place of our own. I have been thinking about it, but not enough I guess. I'm sorry to have caused you such misery."

"Dearest Jonathan," she responded, stroking his chest and looking up into his face with tear filled eyes, "I caused you pain also by the things I said. While some may be true, it was not necessary or kind of me to say them in such a harsh manner. I did see my father today and he offered to let me come home to stay. Though I considered it, I do love you--and so, I told him no."

The relief was instantly visible in Jonathan's face while at the same time, it was evident his curiosity had become piqued.

"How did you see your father? Did your mother change her mind? How did you get there? What did my mother do?"

"I went to my father's office at the bank. No, I do not think my mother has changed her mind, she usually doesn't. I walked to the bus stop, took the bus to the streetcar, and rode the streetcar into town. I simply told your mother I was going into town to get something for you. Jonathan, there is something we must talk about, something I heard about your mother today."

Jonathan's face went ashen as he asked, "What did you hear?"

As Suzanne recounted Sam's comments to Maggie Mae, Jonathan's shoulders slumped as his head fell forward.

He moaned, "I have feared the day would come when you'd learn of this."

Suzanne sat perfectly still, waiting.

"Apparently my mother didn't do well holding down a job. For one thing, there just aren't many jobs available for women who have children and are of a certain age. Also, it seems she would get into scraps with one person or the other when she did manage to find a job. Finally, in desperation, my uncle Gerard offered her a job at his store. However, she walked out after the first day saying it was too much work, too hard on her feet. That is when they first stopped talking, then started talking, then they go mad at each other again and now . . ."

"That is when she turned this house into a 'boarding house' of sorts?"

"Yes."

"Just what sort of boarding house is it, I don't really understand, no one seems to actually live here, right?"

"Suzanne, it is complicated. There are girls who stay here at times for the night, beyond that door at the end of the hallway. They don't stay here for very long, my mother doesn't want to bring attention to the place. She pays the sheriff to look the other way and um . . ."

The reality of the situation was beginning to creep into Suzanne's consciousness and she felt as though she would be violently ill. Her stomach had been slightly upset for several days and Jonathan's words brought it all into focus; she ran fast toward the bathroom.

When she returned, Suzanne said to Jonathan with a steadiness she did not think possible under the circumstances, "We are moving out of here by the end of the week or else I will return home to my parents."

It was much later while lying in bed and looking out the east bay window that Suzanne noticed the bright full moon shining serenely in the velvet night sky. As lacy wisps of clouds floated across the face of the moon, Suzanne's troubled spirit eased into slumber. She was certain Jonathan would find a place for them to live. They would make it into their very own . . . she would reconnect with her friends, and maybe even her family . . . those blue skies Jonathan liked to sing about would appear . . . it would happen, some day, just around the corner.

CHAPTER ELEVEN

It was her birthday today; she was 19 years old. Tears splashed into the basin as she tried one more time to get Jonathan's shirts completely clean.

Shopping and cooking, scrubbing and cleaning, washing clothes and hanging them on the clothesline, all this backbreaking, hard work was still so new to Suzanne. Having a place of one's own took a lot of effort, especially in this ramshackle little cottage. While she was thankful Jonathan's Uncle Gerard had helped them find this place to rent, it was unbelievably tiny and oh so very weather beaten!

While they lived at Maggie Mae's house Suzanne had helped with dinner and she kept their own bedroom clean and tidy. However, Maggie Mae had a laundry woman who came in once a week, a cleaning woman once a month for the heavy work, and several tradesmen who delivered food and other household items such as ice and coal. Further, whenever Suzanne attempted to bring order into the house, Maggie Mae would practically hiss at her,

"You just think you are too good for us, don't you – always

puttin' on the Ritz, ain't ya? Leave my stuff alone. You have your own room to fuss around with . . . don't be messing with my house or my things!"

It helped to have Jonathan working at his uncle's market. She was grateful that every few days he brought groceries home with him--good meat, fresh produce, canned goods, and occasionally left over baked goods. He also took care of getting ice for the icebox, coal for the furnace, and wood for the stove. Additionally, Jonathan was becoming quite handy in the kitchen, his cooking tasted exceptional. Yet, although he was willing to help her out in the kitchen, the rest of the household chores he considered "women's work."

"I am tired when I get home from work and you spend all day here with nothing to do," he replied when Suzanne asked him to help her with the cleaning and the laundry.

"Jonathan, you know I am working hard to make this cottage a nicer place to live. Besides, I seem to get tired more easily than usual and I feel rather sick to my stomach in the mornings. That is why I am asking you to help with the chores, especially the laundry."

"I help you cook the dinner and clean up. I fix anything around here that needs it. I even painted this kitchen sunshine yellow to please you. I come home exhausted from standing on my feel all day, so what I'm doing is enough." Then he softened his tone as he said, "It will get easier, you'll see."

So on and on she scrubbed and cleaned and laundered as

well as arranging and rearranging their things to lighten the drab atmosphere, but it was all so discouraging. Each day, the work started all over again. There was never any time to read or write. There were no flowers in the yard or fields of wild flowers to walk among for respite. In fact, there were no glimpses of beauty to enjoy anywhere outside, at least that she could see. Suzanne felt as though life was slipping away from her.

Suzanne's mind wandered back to her birthday last June. She had just graduated from high school with honors, she was certain she would go to college at some point in the future, and she was extremely excited about all the adventures she planned to experience. She reveled in her dancing dates with Jonathan. Life had been good.

One year later, she was living in poverty. Her dreams of college were dead, she had not seen any of her friends since December; she was estranged from her family. Jonathan was working extra long hours for his uncle and they had not been on a Sunday outing since they moved into this little cottage. She felt bedraggled, bereft, and drained of all hope.

Most of all, something was wrong with her. Her body felt different. She guessed it was time to see a doctor to find out why. Jonathan would have to take her into town next week for a consultation.

As Suzanne finished the laundry and hung it on the line, she noticed a few sprouts in the garden that Jonathan had planted the week they moved in here. Smiling dreamily, she sat down in the only faded green metal chair on the back porch and let the sun wash over her tired body.

Tomorrow, she would talk to Jonathan about planting some flowers along the porch and across the back fence, maybe that would lift her spirits. Tomorrow, she would scrub the hallway floor and hang some of her family photographs on the walls. Tomorrow, she would go out and meet some of their neighbors.

Right now, she let the soothing breezes brushed against her face as she laid her head back and rested, daydreaming about blue birds fluttering through cerulean skies filled with enormous fluffy white clouds.

CHAPTER TWELVE

It was a good thing she had known her doctor for so many years because she certainly did feel uncomfortable today. The time seemed interminable to Suzanne as she waited with Jonathan for the doctor to come in to discuss his findings. Jonathan was fidgeting; she knew that meant he was feeling impatient to be on his way and he was obviously relieved when the doctor entered the room.

"Suzanne, I believe you will find this good news. Though, I am surprised your mother did not help you out with this situation."

Startled, Suzanne replied in confusion, "I am not sure what you mean, Dr. Stevens."

"You are going to have a baby. I estimate it will be born sometime in late November or early December."

"Oh!" was all that Suzanne could manage getting out.

"That's the bee's knees!" whooped Jonathan.

Dr. Stevens smiled benignly at them both and stated, "You will need to return in a month or so, Suzanne, so that I can check your progress."

Bumping along in the roadster toward the cottage, Jonathan

sang *When You're Smiling*, the song recently made famous by Louis Armstrong. Jonathan laughed and talked and sang some more, apparently lost in the joy of the moment.

Suzanne, however, sat very still--her stomach was swirling and her thoughts were chaotic. It was a good thing Jonathan would be leaving right after he dropped her at the cottage, he needed to finish his work day and she needed time alone to adjust to this unexpected news.

After Jonathan left, Suzanne threw herself on the bed and sobbed for a long while. A baby was a precious gift of life and she was angry with herself for crying so. It was just that, she was not quite ready for such an event. Instinctively she knew life was never going to be the same again.

As the sobs subsided, Suzanne took several deep breaths and fell sound asleep. Upon waking, she felt better. The old green metal chair on the back porch seemed like a good place to gather herself and prepare for the time when Jonathan would return. As she walked out the back door, the sky burst into colorful ribbons of raspberry, mango, and lavender as the sun slid toward the horizon. The beauty of the late spring sunset settled her spirit.

"Babies bring love and laughter, and who knows," she reflected, "maybe this baby will also bring my mother around. My father is going to be ecstatic. I will have to find a way to go into town soon so I can tell him. Maybe he can get my mother to soften up and accept Jonathan now."

Humming, Suzanne set the table for dinner. Impulsively,

she ran to the bedroom and dug into her closet looking for something bright to put on--she did not want Jonathan to know how she'd cried over the baby. Her hand brushed the dress she had worn on their wedding day, the one that was daffodil yellow, the one Jonathan admired so very much.

She had just finished changing when Jonathan walked through the front door. Catching a glimpse of her in the bedroom mirror, he rushed in and twirled her round and round.

"We're going to have a baby yes, we're going to have a baby, the most beautiful baby girl, who'll look like her mama--the prettiest girl in town, the dolled up one who is my very own wife."

"What if she is a boy?" Suzanne asked giggling.

"Oh, either one will do, babies are God's gift of love."

Suzanne stopped giggling, surprised at that statement. She had never heard Jonathan talk about God before, but she thought that sounded very nice, babies--a gift of love, from God. That was something she needed to ponder some more.

"May I have this dance, ma'am?" Jonathan asked as he started to whirl Suzanne into a tango. It was great fun, dancing together was something they had not done in a long while.

Stopping very suddenly, he pulled her over to the wing back chair and said breathlessly, "You can't be dancing like that, you are on the nest, and you can't be jumping around like this and jarring the baby. Rest now; I'll go make us dinner."

Suzanne did not really want to stop dancing, but to please Jonathan she sat down and started to read. It was such a pleasure to spend time with one of her beloved books. After several minutes, she relaxed and later daydreamed a bit about the baby.

"Maybe she'll have curly hair and a big charming smile like Jonathan. Maybe her eyes will be large and luminous with long lashes like my father, but blue like Jonathan's eyes. Just maybe, she'll have auburn hair and a spicy personality like me," Suzanne thought saucily, realizing she was thinking of the baby as a girl.

"And maybe, her daddy will take me dancing one more time before I get too clumsy and big," she whispered as she swished her toes back and forth in rhythm to the tune playing on the radio.

By the time Jonathan called her to dinner there was a truly happy smile on her face.

CHAPTER THIRTEEN

The days were getting shorter as Suzanne was getting rounder, though it was still hard to tell she was carrying a baby. The crisp air felt good after the summer heat, which in California lasted well into the fall. Life had settled into a predictable, pleasant pattern of work, along with a bit of pleasure. It was early October of 1929. Suzanne took a break to sit on the porch and look at the last of the fall flowers while she pondered the events of the past few months.

Jonathan was very busy, especially since he had taken a second job delivering ice to a route of customers each weekday well before dawn. Nevertheless, all summer he made certain they spent Sundays relaxing together, saying it was "good for the baby." They had resumed taking long drives through the countryside, going for picnics in the meadow, fishing in the stream, and walking along the easier mountain trails. Suzanne missed dancing together, but was content with the joys of their Sunday adventures.

Many sultry Sunday afternoons found them sprawled out on the bed while Jonathan listened to the baseball game on the radio and Suzanne napped. Jonathan was enamored with the feats of Babe Ruth, following his every move in the daily newspaper. His favorite team, however, remained the Red Sox. In the 1929 World Series, he rooted for the Cubs, though they never recovered after game four when the Athletics made an astounding comeback from an 8-0 deficit to win that game; then went on to win the pennant in game five.

One Saturday night, due to Uncle Gerard's generosity, they had attended Eugene O'Neil's play *Beyond the Horizon* at the Pasadena Playhouse. It was fabulous. Suzanne considered it one of the highlights of her life. All summer they had enjoyed seeing movies together at the local cinema. Jonathan reveled in the antics of Buster Keaton and Laurel and Hardy while Suzanne idolized Mary Pickford, loving the fact that she had her hair bobbed for the movie, *Coquette.*

The cottage was now clean and tidy; it finally felt like home to Suzanne. Jonathan was using some of his extra earnings from his ice route to send out the laundry, saving Suzanne many long hours of backbreaking work.

Their garden provided bountiful fruits and vegetables all summer long. Long rows filled with Mason jars of tomatoes, corn relish, pickles, and strawberry and blackberry preserves along with canned peaches and pears lined the pantry shelves. Their neighbor with the prolific fruit trees had been overjoyed to trade some of her crop for theirs. Jonathan made corn relish and even canned some stewed tomatoes, which Suzanne found quite tasty, but caused her to query,

"Where'd you learn to do such things?"

To which Jonathan replied, "I'm really a farm boy, remember? Learned lots of stuff from my daddy about growing things and such. Back in those days, my mother used to cook and sew, and can and smoke meat and do all the things a farmer's wife does. She taught me some of 'em, though she says now that she hated it all . . . doesn't want to think about it anymore. But, me, well, doing those things makes me feel warm and contented inside . . . like I'm a boy again and things are safe and happy still . . . I'm sure glad I found you, Suzy girl. You're the best thing that ever happened to me!"

Suzanne giggled and stroked his cheek before she kissed him soundly and long.

Jonathan ducked his head and grinned, "Maybe after the baby is born, we'll try our hand at keepin' chickens."

Suzanne was not so sure she liked that idea, yet she was certainly grateful that Grandmother Stuart had taught her the art of canning. She recalled vividly the day her mother had queried sharply, "Mom, why are you teaching Suzanne to make pickles and jam? Canning is cook's job. Suzanne certainly does not need to cultivate such a skill."

Grandmother Stuart had replied firmly, "One never knows when economy will be needed in life. It won't hurt Suzanne to learn how to do this."

Every week or so, Jonathan brought her a new book to read. The Pasadena Central Library was located close enough to the market for Jonathan to slip over to it during lunch break. Suzanne was especially grateful for this diversion, as she had now become too obviously "in the family way" to appear in public. Grandmother Stuart had also attempted to teach her to knit and do needlework, but those skills never took with Suzanne. Besides, she would rather read or listen to the radio.

Although her father was elated over the news about the baby, he told her that Grace continued to stand her ground stating that Suzanne and Jonathan would never again be allowed to visit nor did she wish to speak of them.

"What makes my mother so stubborn and spiteful?" Suzanne would often ponder, and then with a jut of her chin would resolve, "No matter, Jonathan loves me, we are always going to live happily together, and our baby is going to make us into a real family."

Jonathan's brother, Danny, came home for several weeks on leave from the Navy. His ship was leaving for a long tour; they would not see him again for almost a year. He was a shorter, less gregarious version of Jonathan. Nevertheless, it had been a delight to make his acquaintance. Even Maggie Mae had been on her best behavior during their dinners together.

It was a resplendent fall afternoon when her old friend Tom came by with his new wife, Cassandra. They had a delightful visit. Recalling stories of their childhood and youth brought them all into fresh bouts of laughter every few minutes. Oh, how good it was to see Tom! While Suzanne was well aware that her home was not the impressive manor of her parents, she was proud of what Jonathan and she had accomplished in making the old cottage into a cozy home. Tom simply wanted to know if she was happy. She assured him that she was, especially with their baby coming soon.

Dr. Stevens was certain all was well with the pregnancy. He said while she was sedated the delivery would be easily accomplished. Even so, Suzanne was rather terrified at the prospect. She would most certainly be glad when it was all over and their precious baby was safely resting in the little white enameled crib Jonathan had set up in their bedroom.

The evenings were getting chilly, and this Thursday evening, the 24th of October, Jonathan dozed in the wing back chair, listening to Amos 'n' Andy on the radio as Suzanne sat reading by the fire. A newscaster cut into the show to announce that the share prices on the New York Stock Exchange had collapsed during the day, causing a domino effect that was now being felt in Europe as it was starting its Friday morning business day. Suzanne glanced over at Jonathan to see what he thought of the announcement. As he did not seem to react, she went back to reading *Roper's Row.*

Monday night when Jonathan came home from work, he recounted to Suzanne his uncle's uneasy behavior over the stock market events.

"It really is not something to concern us, though, is it Jonathan?" Suzanne asked with a slight feeling of fear.

"I don't see why it would," Jonathan replied. "Everyone

needs to shop at the market for their groceries. Uncle Gerard has been flush all summer. That raise he gave me in August means I won't have to deliver ice anymore after we've paid off everything for the baby. I don't think we have a worry in the world. It's just one of those things that happen on Wall Street."

On Tuesday afternoon, the radio announcer cut in while Suzanne was listening to Louie Armstrong singing on the radio-- stating in a sonorous voice, "Stock prices collapsed again today. People everywhere are in a panic; they can't get rid of their stocks fast enough."

Right after that unsettling announcement, Edward stopped by to say that Grandfather Hughes' bank had closed early for the day after it had been hit by a run. He had been rather flippant, "Maybe Dad will get to stay home now and tend the orchards like he's always wanted to do."

Then seeing Suzanne's fear, he quickly reasoned, "Oh, you know grandfather. He's sharp; he's got everything under control. Everything will be copacetic, I'm sure of it."

The baby was moving restlessly in response to Suzanne's panic. After Edward left, she drew the shades, laid down and tried to rest. Even though she tired easily these days, it was so awfully hard to get comfortable. Soon after, Jonathan appeared in the doorway--home early from work.

"Uncle Gerard's been in a terrible panic. He says he bought stocks on a margin, whatever that is, hoping he'd get rich quick. He was pacing and practically screaming at everyone. He decided to close the store early and sent everyone home. He was certain people would panic, come empty the shelves, but then not pay their bill at the end of the month. He's acted crazy all day. I was happy to just get out of there!"

"Jonathan, what will we do if something happens to your job at the store? The baby is due next month."

"Oh, nothing to worry about, I'll just go find another job. I'll always take care of you my darlin'. Besides, I think Uncle Gerard is simply overreacting. How could a grocery store in California be affected by a few problems with the stock market in New York?" Jonathan replied as he rubbed her swollen feet. "Remember, for us it's going to be skies of blue and days of sunshine. I'm not going to let anything happen to you or that baby girl we've dreamed about all summer long.

Suzanne slowly relaxed as Jonathan massaged her back while he whistled the tune *Side By Side.* Leave it to Jonathan to think about that song right now. It was a song loved by them both and seemed especially applicable for their circumstances.

"Surely, he's right," she mused, feeling refreshed and ready to start cooking their dinner. "What's happening all the way over in New York City has very little to do with us."

Then irreverently she thought, "It's going to be awfully funny to see a little boy dressed up like the little girl Jonathan is sure we're having."

December, 1929
Glendora, California

CHAPTER FOURTEEN

Four days after Thanksgiving, Suzanne woke to sharp pains flitting across her tummy, which she decided must be the labor pains Dr. Stevens had described. Unfortunately, Jonathan had left several hours ago to deliver ice to his customers.

"It's a good thing we have a backup plan," she thought, scurrying around the cold bedroom looking for her slippers. "It's also a good thing that I decided to pack my bag for the hospital this weekend, just in case. Otherwise, I would most certainly forget something important in my haste and worry to get there fast!"

Dressed and ready to go, Suzanne carefully walked with bag in hand next door to the Kline's house. Mary and Harvey had promised long ago that they would get Suzanne to the hospital if Jonathan was not available.

"They are such lovely people, it is a shame they never could have children," Suzanne thought as she rang the doorbell.

Three rings later, Harvey groggily answered the door.

"Oh, heavens, you're here. Mary, come right now, we're leaving for the hospital! Suzanne is outside," he yelled, running for the bedroom.

"Better let her come in and sit down," Mary yelled back.

"Oh, Suzanne, forgive me. I wasn't thinking, come in, sit down. Let me carry that," Harvey excitedly told her, out of breath from the sudden exertion.

Jostling along the rutted road in Harvey's old jalopy several minutes later, Suzanne was not certain she could endure the ride into town. Each bounce brought another intense stab of pain. Oh, how she wished for Jonathan right now.

"How are we going to get word to him?" she pondered. Uncle Gerard never answered his phone until mid-morning when customers started calling in orders to be delivered later in the day.

"Now, honey, once we get you settled at the hospital, I'll just drive right over to the market and leave word for Jonathan to get over here soon as he gets in from his ice route."

Suzanne was relieved.

"You sit right down here while we call the doctor," the nurse said soothingly once they arrived. "We'll get you into a room right quick, don't you worry now girlie, we'll take good care of you. Now, where's your husband? He was right here a minute ago."

"Oh, that's not my husband, that's my neighbor," Suzanne replied, sinking into the nearest chair just as another contraction hit her unexpectedly.

"I see," said the nurse with a disapproving frown on her face.

"My husband left for work early this morning. My neighbor brought me here then went to fetch him."

"Ah, I see," said the nurse, her face clearing of its frown.

Many hours later, Suzanne delivered a healthy baby girl with blond fuzz and blue eyes. Jonathan was ecstatic. He carried her all around the hospital, showing off his "precious bundle of joy" to anyone who would look and listen.

"You'd think he was the first man who ever had a baby girl." Suzanne thought as she drifted off to sleep. "Hope those nurses rescue her soon, she needs to rest too. I do hope my father comes to see me."

When Suzanne awoke, her father stood by her bedside, beaming.

"Suzie girl, I am overjoyed! Thankfully, you are doing well as is the baby. What will you name her?"

"We have not talked about that yet, father. It is so good to see you." Suzanne replied, holding his hand tightly in hers. "Will you tell mother about the baby?"

"Of course she has been curious to know how you are doing. I think she is thawing just a little. She is concerned about you, though she'd never admit it to anyone. Edward seems pleased also."

Suzanne eyes welled up, her heart feeling slightly hopeful as Jonathan walked in with the baby.

"Hello, sir. Meet your granddaughter. Baby girl, smile for your grandpa."

This comment brought an enchanted smile to her father's face as he reached out for the baby. Suzanne lay back content.

The next morning they decided on a name – Rose Anne Kelly.

"Baby girl, I am going to call you Rosie, you are my precious Rosie doll and your birthday is December 2, 1929. You'll remember that now, won't you?" Jonathan cooed at the baby.

Although at first Suzanne thought him a little silly, she was secretly relieved that he was so very happy to have a girl when so many men wanted to have boys for their first child.

"Where is Grace?" many a nurse stopped by to ask, making the pain of her absence ever so hard for Suzanne. Even though her mother volunteered at the hospital once a week, she never came by to see her new baby granddaughter.

Maggie Mae came twice. Suzanne gritted her teeth and acted as graciously as she knew how under the circumstances. It seemed rather strange that each time, Maggie Mae spent a long time all alone with Jonathan outside Suzanne's room, and just a few minutes with baby Rose. But then, Suzanne thought her altogether odd anyway.

Once home, they settled quickly into the routine of family life. Rosie cried a lot those first couple of weeks. Jonathan was considerate of Suzanne's weakened state and lack of sleep. He cooked every meal and often held Rosie on his lap so Suzanne could rest. However, he still would not do "women's chores" and Suzanne was getting desperate about the lack of cleanliness in their erstwhile tidy home.

Fortunately, several days later Mary and Harvey stopped by to see the baby and Mary immediately saw the situation for what it was.

"I'll just come over tomorrow and help you put things in ship shape," Mary softly told Suzanne when Jonathan went into the kitchen to get everyone a cup of coffee.

"That would be a great relief," Suzanne quickly replied. "Thank you!"

October's distressing news about stocks and banks seemed far, far away from their cozy little cottage. Besides President Hoover said to the nation in the Thanksgiving Proclamation he gave on November 5, 1929, that:

> *God has greatly blessed us as a nation in the year now drawing to a close. The earth has yielded an abundant harvest in most parts of our country. The fruits of industry have been of unexampled quantity and value. Both capital and labor have enjoyed an exceptional prosperity.*

Suzanne was confident that Uncle Gerard had his business affairs in order and as such, Jonathan's job was secure. Jonathan planned to work a couple more months on the ice route so they could put a little away for the future. However, she would be ever so happy when he could go back to just working at the market. She would find ways to economize so they would not miss the extra money.

Certainly one of these days her mother's stubbornness

would recede and she would come to see her first grandchild or better yet, invite Jonathan and Suzanne to be part of the family gatherings again. Suzanne wished to see her grandparents, cousins, aunts, and uncles once more, she missed them all terribly.

When Rose was a little older, Suzanne intended to find a way to renew her friendship with Louise and maybe some of her other childhood friends. Mary had already offered to babysit little Rosie when Suzanne was ready to leave her. Suzanne planned to get out in the world again as soon as possible; she missed dancing, their Sunday adventures, and oh, so many other fun things.

"They'll all see, Jonathan and you and me are going to be happy together always," she would tell Rosie as they sat rocking in the chair her beloved grandmother and grandfather Hughes had sent over from Barker Brothers in Los Angeles. While Suzanne sang a nursery song to her about cats and mice dancing together, little Rose Anne Kelly slept on, peacefully content.

CHAPTER FIFTEEN

By December 23rd the baby had finally settled into a semi-predictable pattern of eating and sleeping, while Suzanne was rapidly regaining her energy level and petite waistline.

When the doorbell rang, Suzanne assumed it was Mary, her neighbor, coming over to help with the housework. Instead, her mother Grace stood rigidly on the front porch. Speechless, Suzanne simply stood and waited, not knowing exactly what to expect.

"Are you not going to invite me into your home?" her mother asked in her usual brusque manner, leaving Suzanne feeling rather weak and shaky.

"Of course, Mother, come in, sit down. Can I bring you some tea or coffee or something?" Suzanne responded in trepidation.

"No, I did not come to use up your resources. I came to ask if you would like to join us for Christmas dinner. I would also like to see that granddaughter of mine, if I may."

"Of course, Mother, you may see Rosie. Actually, her name is Rose Anne. She is sleeping, but will soon wake up for a feeding.

It is good to see you." Suzanne replied, feeling cautious.

"About Christmas dinner, I will most certainly ask Jonathan. I imagine he will be fine with it. I would love to see everyone, I have missed them." Suzanne continued as tears formed in the corners of her eyes.

"Very well, I expect you can give me an answer soon." Grace stated stiffly looking around the tiny cottage. "You do seem to have a clean house for having no help and a new baby."

"Thank you Mother. My neighbor, Mary, has been helping. Jonathan does too, when he can. It is a surprise to see you."

"I know. Everyone at the hospital has been aghast that I have not seen your baby. My friends have been telling me to let bygones be bygones and of course, your father . . . you know, he is such a tender, forgiving soul. Mind you, I still do not approve. However, now that you have a baby, it does look like Jonathan is here to stay. Truthfully, I have missed you." Grace said, almost wistfully before she stiffened up again.

Suzanne could not hide her astonishment.

"Oh mother, yes, I am so glad you came. Rosie needs her grandmother and I . . . I . . . it was hard to have a baby without you."

Immediately, Suzanne knew she had said the wrong thing.

"You should have thought of that when you ran off and got married. This was your choice not mine."

Instead of taking her usual fighting stance, Suzanne softly replied, "I realize that mother. Let's not let that stand between us any more, for Rosie's sake."

Fortuitously, Rosie chose that exact moment to cry. Grace, visibly excited, walked with Suzanne to the bedroom and met her granddaughter for the first time. Holding the baby, Grace appeared almost happy as a smile endeavored to burst through her stern demeanor. Suzanne relaxed a bit and led them all back to sit on the davenport together.

When baby Rose appeared to look up at her, Grace gently kissed her tiny cheek, while softly telling her, "I held your mama like this once. She was the most beautiful baby you have ever seen. She grew into a beautiful woman and now, you are her beautiful little baby."

Again, Suzanne could not hide her astonishment.

"I am happy that you think so, mother. Jonathan and I are very proud of her. She's a very good baby. Jonathan loves her, and me, very very much."

Once again, Grace stiffened as she replied, "Well, he certainly went about everything the wrong way. What does he do for a living anyway? Is he going to be able to make his way in the world, care for this baby and you?"

"Yes, mother, Jonathan works very hard at his uncle's market. He also works at a second job, delivering ice to people for their iceboxes. We have all that we truly need."

"Hum! That does not seem like much of a living to me. But, I am grateful to see you are not wallowing in total poverty, though, this house is rather small and old. Nothing like you could have had. You should have married someone of your own kind, someone from our social circle. However--and mind you, I still do not approve of your choices--you now have a child; the deed is done and cannot be undone."

Marriage and motherhood had tempered Suzanne's saucy temperament a bit; she merely nodded, "Yes, mother, our little Rosie is here, let's enjoy her together."

Grace went right on holding onto Rosie who rested contentedly in her arms. Suzanne fully expected her mother to briskly hand the baby back and leave, after all, she was always so very busy. Instead, she actually appeared to be enjoying the baby!

In spite of her mother's protestations, Suzanne knew that she would enjoy a cup of jasmine tea, so went to the kitchen to prepare it. She returned to find her mother bent over Rosie, making cooing noises and talking soothingly to her while Rosie lay in her arms, relaxed and quiet.

Suzanne's astonishment grew with each passing moment.

Relating the scene to Jonathan later that evening, Suzanne continued to marvel.

"Jonathan, I do not ever remember seeing my mother like that, except for maybe in the picture my parents have from their honeymoon. In it my mother looks absolutely giddy and my father has a big goofy smile on his face. She said my father read poetry to her every day and he strummed on a guitar while singing love songs to her. I have never seen either one of them act like that, besides my mother's face only has one setting--stern."

"Oh, she just needs to have a good laugh," Jonathan said lightly.

"Let's go for Christmas dinner, please! I do so want to see my grandparents and cousins again." Suzanne begged.

"Of course we'll go, honey girl," Jonathan responded. "We'll all have a grand time together. You'll see."

Having her mother and Jonathan in the same room for more than a few minutes might prove to be disastrous; Jonathan had never been on the receiving end of one of Grace's diatribes. Nevertheless, Suzanne was willing to try. Christmas Day seemed the perfect opportunity to mend fences; after all, it was a day set aside for families, gifts, and other such delights.

CHAPTER SIXTEEN

"What a dreary day!" Suzanne told Jonathan as he prepared to leave for his job at the market. He'd quit his job delivering ice and now left the house at a decent hour. Although she tried to sleep a little longer this morning, Rosie was fussing again. Rosie had been up in the night, crying every hour or so. Smoky grey clouds hung over everything like a loosely knit blanket, making the day feel ominous and sad. Suzanne herself felt sad, sleepy, rather sick to her stomach, and slightly out of sorts.

"Rosie girl, I don't like January, especially when the weather gets so ugly. It's a dreary month with dreary clouds and rain. I like Christmas with the lights and the tree and the tinsel and the cheery Christmas songs. That's it--we'll put on the radio."

When Suzanne turned on the radio, Fats Waller had just started singing *Ain't Misbehavin',* bringing a smile to her face.

Music had a way of making Suzanne feel all was right with world again. She should have been feeling fine, after all the merriment of Christmas day and seeing her family again. They had all loved Jonathan with his boisterous jokes and big easy grin.

Well, that is, everyone except her mother. Grace just could not let go of her disappointment about the marriage and Jonathan's lack of social polish; simply put, Grace never could hide her feelings, especially when she was irritated. Every time Grace would look at Jonathan, she would tense up and frown. Her father, Charles, quickly caught on that Rosie made all the difference to the situation. As such, Rosie spent a great deal of time with her grandmother Grace that day.

"Actually," Suzanne mused, "it went far better than I ever expected."

She had been relieved to overhear her grandfather Hughes telling the uncles on her mother's side that all was smoothing out at the bank after the disasters of October and November. Christmas dinner was as sumptuous as ever and her family had lavished Rosie Anne with gifts. Rosie's drawers were now overflowing with clothes and she even had a little stash of toys that she would enjoy one of these days. Her uncle Edward bought her a pair of cowboy boots, tiny red ones. Although it would be many, many months before Rosie could wear them, Suzanne found the sight of them sitting on the shelf quite amusing. Leave it to her brother to buy something so impractical for a baby that was just a few weeks old.

Rosie ate, and then slept for almost three hours. Suzanne napped along with her. When she woke, she felt better. However, the dark, grey clouds still lingered outside.

Suzanne was just starting to prepare dinner when Jonathan came up behind her, sweeping her into his arms and startling her.

He was home early again from work, this time looking weary and worried. She shivered slightly, something told her he had bad news; she'd felt all along there was something not quite right about this day.

"What's wrong Jonathan, you are here early. Did something go wrong again at the store?"

Jonathan sighed, "Yep, something's wrong. Uncle Gerard told me today that he is closing the store."

"Closing the store?"

"Why?"

"When?"

"What is he thinking?" she practically shouted.

"He says he lost almost everything when the stocks fell. His real estate is all mortgaged up, including the store. Worst of all, since that stock market crash in late October people have been cutting back on their purchases and some are not paying the monthly tab they've run up, they're saying they can't afford it. Uncle Gerard says he's going to Arizona . . . he's keeps on saying, 'Arizona is the place to be--its cheaper and not so crowded."

"You mean he's mortgaged your mother's house?"

"No, he says that's not mortgaged. He's putting her house in my name and Danny's, too, along with the stipulation that we make certain my mother always has a place to live. He feels bad about doing this to you and me and that I am losing my job, but he says I am young and strong and I'll make my way."

Finding the nearest chair, Suzanne sat down in silence

wondering what they would do now. She felt so helpless. It felt like they were just a pair of blue birds, flapping in the wind, in a whirlwind of bad fortune.

"I stopped at the ice warehouse and they were thrilled to have me take back my route. I'll ask around town tomorrow, see what's out there. It's a good thing we've put a little away in the strong box for emergencies. Uncle Gerard is staying open for two more weeks, hoping to collect as much due him as possible. Then he's going to announce that he's closing and he'll see if he can sell off the fixtures and such, but he doubts it, times are getting tough. He says I can work until the very last day. He's going to give us as many staple goods as we think we can manage to store here."

"I am sorry you have to get up so early again, but that is good news about the ice route. Maybe you can build some extra shelves in the pantry or we can find another place in the house to store Uncle Gerard's staple goods. We'll have to just cut back on our expenses, some way or another."

"Suzie girl, I am sorry, you do realize this means we'll have to stop sending out the laundry, you're going to have to find a way to do it--the most important thing of all is paying the rent and keeping the household running."

With a sigh of discouragement, Suzanne replied, "Yes, I do realize. It doesn't matter, I am young and strong. I'll make it too."

As he often did at such times, Jonathan broke into song as he waltzed Suzanne around the kitchen, singing Irving Berlin's enchanting love song *Always*. Baby Rose awoke, so Jonathan scooped her up and putting her between them, continued their dance as the gloomy day slid into a misty dusk.

They talked late into the night, making plans for economizing while holding each other in a tight grip of intense love that was interlinked with gut-wrenching fear.

Later, when Suzanne got up to feed Rosie, she realized Jonathan was not on his side of the bed. She assumed he was in the kitchen or reading by the fire. Sometimes, he liked to do that.

The next morning, he was groggy and grumpy. He also smelled of stale beer. Before she could ask though, he was gone to work. Once again, she was feeling slightly sick to her stomach.

"Must be all the emotional upheaval of yesterday," Suzanne told herself as she went about the chores of the day. She was relieved that Rose had returned to her usual placid self, leaving Suzanne free to sort out her turbulent emotions.

April, 1930
Glendora, California

CHAPTER SEVENTEEN

Though she tried to dodge the truth of the matter, Suzanne was almost certain that baby Rose would be joined by a sibling before the year 1930 ended. It was too soon. She was not at all prepared for such an event. Nevertheless, with each day that passed, the facts became ever more irrefutable. Jonathan was going to have to be told. Working three part time jobs was keeping them going, but he was constantly worn-out. News of another baby would most certainly create more tension between them.

Her news, however, had the opposite effect on Jonathan; to her complete surprise he was ecstatic at the thought of having another child.

"We'll have a little boy this time. Goin' to name him Jonathan, after me. We can call him Johnny. He'll grow up to be a fine man, make us proud."

Suzanne felt overwhelmed. Jonathan did not seem to grasp the work involved or the cost.

"Oh, Suzie girl," he laughed at her concerns. "We'll make it through. We're young and strong. Babies are the best news there is in the world. Remember how you worried over having Rosie. Just think of all the delight she's brought us."

It was true, each day that passed; Rosie brought them more joy than Suzanne had dreamed was even possible. At almost five months old baby Rose was already showing signs of a charming temperament. Another wave of nausea sent Suzanne scurrying for the bathroom. It seemed much worse this time.

"How will I care for Rosie, keep up with the laundry and housework as well as preparing economic meals when I feel this poorly?" Suzanne fretted. For once in her life, she longed for her mother's efficient energy and for the first time in a long time, she longed for the ease of her former life.

Grace and Charles were scheduled for a visit to see Rosie on Saturday. Suzanne had invited them to stay for dinner. Her mother had firmly refused. She never really understood her mother's reticence over such things. She knew her father would enjoy the visit and would want to stay as long as possible, but she also knew that once it was made up, there was no changing Grace's mind. Her parents would have to be told before the facts became too obvious. Yet, Suzanne dreaded her mother's caustic comments.

When informed her mother retorted, "Is that so," exhibiting her usual disapproval, "and is Jonathan prepared to care for this child with no real job, no actual home of your own, and no apparent prospects?"

"Mother," Suzanne spoke wearily, "Jonathan works very

hard and we have never gone without. Do you not see that Rosie is thriving?"

"Of course she is thriving, she is a Hughes and a Stuart. Rose Anne comes from a long line of sturdy, intelligent, industrious people. Jonathan got lucky finding a treasure like you to bear his children."

"Grace," Charles interposed, "Jonathan is Rosie's father, you must not be so disparaging of him. This is a fine little home for them to start life together in, and Jonathan has proven himself to be a hard worker. You must give him credit for that."

"We will talk of it no more. Where is Rosie? We came to see her," her mother replied, as usual avoiding any further conversation about things she could not control.

Her father would pay for his remarks, of that Suzanne was certain. Next time they were alone, she would thank him for his gesture of love and affirmation. As usual, it did not appear that she would receive any emotional support from her mother.

After they left, Suzanne sat for a long while on the back porch, playing with Rosie and drinking in the beauty of the spring flowers that were blossoming profusely. Jonathan's garden was bigger this year; he said they needed the produce for their meals. In spite of all his busyness, he still tended the garden regularly-- weeding, fertilizing from his compost pile, clipping off stems to encourage growth, and diligently watering when the sun shone bright. She was grateful that he considered her flowers and shrubs important too; they brought her such joy!

"Rosie my girl, what do you think of having a baby brother or sister in this house? You'll be the big sister. You are still just a baby though and, it does not seem fair to put you in that role already. You are going to have to grow up fast. Mama's going to be so busy." Suzanne whispered as the tears spilled over and into Rose's hair while Rosie happily buried her head into her mother's shoulder.

As spring turned into summer, Suzanne's queasiness dispelled giving her renewed energy. Rosie was crawling and exploring, keeping Suzanne engaged in a battle with dirt and questionable objects which constantly found their way into Rosie's mouth. She was ever grateful for the ongoing help provided by her neighbors, Mary and Harvey.

Many warm summer days found Mary and Suzanne hanging laundry together as the radio played through the kitchen window with Harvey tending Rosie playing alongside. Harvey often shared entertaining tales from his days in the army during the Great War while Mary told of her childhood in France. They met early on after Harvey was stationed over there and they'd married shortly after meeting. After all these years, it was obvious that they were still madly in love with each other. It gave Suzanne great hope for her life with Jonathan as she certainly did not want to end up as angry as her parents seemed to be with each other.

Not able to have children of their own, Mary and Harvey were overjoyed at the news about Suzanne's second pregnancy. They quickly assured her of their support, promising their help to get through it and telling her to plan on canning days and other such work parties involving their helpful hands and tender loving care.

This relieved Suzanne a great deal, though she longed for her former comparative ease and the amusements she'd spent with Jonathan. Once again, due to his busyness and her ever expanding frame, their Sunday adventures had gone by the wayside.

As the heat of late summer enveloped them, Suzanne seemed to grow tired very quickly. Her mother scolded her about eating heartily for the baby's sake. She was trying, however, to conserve so they could pay for the new baby. Jonathan was working at jobs that required so much physical labor that he often fell asleep long before his beloved baseball games were finished, leaving Suzanne to carry the entire load for Rosie's care in the evening.

It was a chilly morning in late September when, right after leaving for his ice route, Jonathan unexpectedly limped back into the house.

"Fell asleep at the wheel, crashed the ice truck into a tree, not sure what they'll say at the icehouse, but I need you to drive me into town in so I can tell 'em, this leg of mine won't work the clutch right now." Jonathan said as he collapsed, head back, into a kitchen chair, revealing a bloody gash in his forehead. Suzanne barely had it cleaned up before he shouted that they had to go.

Suzanne hurriedly threw on some appropriate clothes, bundled up little Rosie, and the three of them drove off in the ancient roadster.

"Jonathan, it's tough times ya' know. You've cost us a bundle wrecking that truck like you did. I'm goin' t' haft' ta let you go. It's not my decision, it's the boss man. He's furious, says we can't be losin' money like that," the supervisor practically shouted, trying not to stare at Suzanne's large rounded belly.

They drove along in absolute silence. They were almost home before Suzanne ventured, "Maybe my father can help until we have the baby."

"I will not crawl to your father for help. You, Rosie and the new baby are my responsibility and I'll thank you to stay out of it." Jonathan said harshly.

His harshness was more than Suzanne could bear after the shock of Jonathan's accident, the hasty drive into town, and the accompanying bad news. The tears flowed uncontrollably.

"I'm so sorry, hon. I shouldn't have done that. Pull over so I can take over and get us home."

As they made their way through town, it was obvious the pain in his leg was excruciating and they both feared it was broken.

"We must go see the doctor," Suzanne insisted.

"It'll cost too much," Jonathan retorted.

"No more than it will cost if you have a bum leg for the rest of your life," she replied decidedly.

Nevertheless, it was several hours before Jonathan gave up in desperation and allowed Suzanne to drive him back into town. Fortunately, the leg was not broken, just badly bruised. The doctor said it should heal up in a few days. He told Jonathan to stay off the leg, use ice on it, and handed him a prescription for pain medication; however, Jonathan would not fill it, saying it cost too much money and what was wrong with that "damned doctor" anyway! Jonathan's angry demeanor scared Rosie and she started to cry. Suzanne felt desperate and alone; she had no idea how to make Jonathan stop his shouting and cursing.

They both feared that because he missed his shift at the lumber yard, it would cost Jonathan his job and it did. Once again the foreman said they were sorry, but it was due to tough times and that they were about to let him go anyway due to poor business. When she heard the news, Suzanne started shaking with uncontrollable chills, resulting from all the pent up anxiety. She feared this would cause the baby to come too early and told Jonathan that she needed to lie down immediately. It was hard to rest. All she could think about was that here they were again, flapping around like little blue birds, trying to buck up against the winds of misfortune. When Suzanne finally heard Jonathan and Rosie playing horsie in the living room, she was able to calm herself and drift off to sleep.

In a daze, they made it through the next couple of weeks, wondering just what they would do. The baby was due in early November and they still had the hospital to pay besides all their usual household expenses. The staples they had received from Uncle Gerard when he closed the store were dwindling, though they had the summer's bounty canned and sitting on the panty shelves in a beautiful display of vivid colors. The strong box had some money in it; however it did not contain enough to carry them through with just one part time job and a new baby on its way.

Suzanne knew her father's groves would need extra hands for the harvest season. She urged Jonathan at least to ask her father about that possibility. Since it would not involve taking charity from her family, Jonathan did so and those wages carried them for a few more weeks. Once the harvest was finished, Jonathan insisted he was finished too, vehement that he would not presume upon his father-in-law's good will.

In a weakened state, on November 8th, Suzanne delivered Jonathan Patrick Kelly, Jr.

Little Johnny did not cry out as lustily as had Rosie Anne, while Suzanne was too exhausted and weak to even notice.

CHAPTER EIGHTEEN

Once again, Jonathan carried the baby all over the hospital, showing off his newborn son with such pride that almost the entire hospital staff was soon reveling in their offspring. Suzanne was exhausted and fearful for the baby's health.

Brushing aside her concerns, Jonathan said with gusto, "Babies are meant to be enjoyed and the delight of them shared."

Too tired to argue, Suzanne rolled over and quickly fell asleep. The delivery had robbed her of all strength. Though she had been extremely tired last time, she did not remember feeling this drained. After sleeping for several hours, Suzanne woke to once again find her father by her side. This time, however, her mother had joined him.

"It was too soon for another baby, of course, but I congratulate you on the birth of your son. You have one of each now, a boy and a girl. It is time to stop having children," Grace stated, as always expecting to be obeyed without question.

Holding back a biting retort, Suzanne simply responded,

"Did you know we named the baby Jonathan Patrick Kelly, Jr.?"

"No," her mother responded brusquely, "I was hoping for a name from our side of the family, maybe my family name, Stuart or . . . or Charles for your father."

"Mother, it is Jonathan's first son and he wanted him to carry his name."

"That is not unusual, by any means," her dear father interjected before Grace could register a further complaint.

When Jonathan returned to Suzanne's room carrying little Johnny, her parents spent a bit of time with the baby, yet left quickly soon after.

"Jonathan, do you think my mother will ever be truly happy over anything?"

"She adores little Rosie. When she sees her, it is the closest she comes to smiling. One day when she was visiting, I caught her actually laughing right out loud at Rosie's antics. I think we should ask your parents to take Rosie home for a few days to visit. It would be good for them both and give you a better rest."

"But Jonathan dear, Mary and Harvey were so overjoyed to take her when we came to the hospital."

"That's true hon, but they see her almost every day. It would be good for your mother and your father. Let's ask them."

As Jonathan predicted, her parents were ecstatic at being asked to care for Rosie. One week turned into three due to Suzanne's poor rate of recovery. Her parents dutifully brought little Rose for a visit every few days so she could get to know little Johnny and see Suzanne.

It was obvious that Jonathan missed Rosie terribly, but everyone was troubled by Suzanne's lack of strength, so it was agreed to continue the arrangement into a fourth week. Suzanne was ever grateful for the continued help supplied by their good neighbors.

By the second week of December, Suzanne developed a cough that racked her body with convulsions. Dr. Stevens diagnosed pneumonia and ordered her admitted to the hospital. She had grown too weak to nurse baby Johnny, so Mary and Harvey took over, introducing him to the bottle and caring for his needs. Charles and Grace took Rosie home to stay with them until Suzanne returned to good health. Suzanne was dimly aware that Jonathan was bereft, but she was altogether too woozy to comfort him.

One evening, through a haze, Suzanne realized that Dr. Stevens was having a heated exchange with her mother over his proposed treatment using antipneumococcal antiserum. Her mother was fearful it would take Suzanne's life, while Dr. Steven's was adamant she might not live unless it was administered. Fortunately, Jonathan appeared, having finished his work for the day, to approve Dr. Steven's plan, which started Suzanne on her road to recovery.

Christmas was a quiet celebration wherein everyone realized how close they came to losing Suzanne. Even Grace went out of her way to bring about good cheer, acquiescing to Suzanne's wishes for a peaceful day without rancor towards Jonathan.

As the year 1931 approached, Suzanne continued to recuperate, slowly regaining strength, and thankful that baby Johnny was such a placid baby. However, she was most fearful about their financial future. Jonathan was working one part time job along with taking odd jobs whenever possible.

Her father had recently confided quietly to Suzanne that the hospital and doctor's bills had been covered by her maternal grandparents and uncles as a gift of love with no expectations for reimbursement. Charles had arranged for the hospital and doctor to simply tell Jonathan that a wealthy patron of the hospital had covered the bill. This arrangement relieved many of Suzanne's fears as she was well aware that Jonathan would not knowingly accept charity from her family.

The glories of Christmas and the enchantment of a new year were quickly replaced by the gloom of January. Cloudy day upon cloudy day often brought heavy rainfall to the area. In vain, Jonathan stood in line after line of frantic workers seeking a decent job--all to no avail.

Desperate as the month ended, unable to pay the rent or catch up with their unpaid bills, Jonathan packed up the family and moved everyone to his mother's house.

Suzanne was devastated at the loss of their cozy cottage, their prolific garden, their delightful neighbors, and their treasured privacy. Once again, she felt as though they were simply a pair of bluebirds, flapping frantically against the wind as they tried to care for two small children.

"It is only temporary, Suzanne my love. I will find a decent paying job soon and we will get back on our feet. I promise." Jonathan told her, sounding much less sure of himself than he realized.

Within the week, Jonathan's brother, Danny arrived home with a new bride, Molly to introduce to the family. The old place was filled with chaotic bustle as Suzanne tried to keep up with fourteen month old Rosie and baby Johnny while Danny and Molly adjusted to married life.   As usual, Maggie Mae snarled and snapped at everyone, especially Suzanne, making Suzanne's life a misery when she was present. Molly appeared positively terrified of the woman.

Though not yet twenty-one years old, Suzanne felt she had become a haggard old caricature of herself.

"Things could not possibly be any worse! Where will we all end up? How long will it be before Jonathan finds a job like the one he had with Uncle Gerard? Am I stuck here forever?" Suzanne would muse as she went about her daily chores, trying not to let anyone see how discouraged she was or that she dreaded the future.

Though he was trying hard to keep up a good front, she knew that Jonathan was also worried about their future. However, he generally hid his uneasiness behind a cocksure approach to life.

Suzanne recalled one Saturday morning, as they were walking along Grand Avenue pushing baby Rosie in a stroller, an older man approached with his wife, looking every bit the self-satisfied, over-refined, stuffy business man that he was. He looked the very young family up and down, then blurted out, "Young man, how did you ever get such large feet? They are quite oversized for your body."

Without hesitation, Jonathan replied, "So when I get old and fat like you, I'll have something to hold up my big old belly."

In a huff, the man hurried on while Jonathan laughed convulsively.

"Jonathan! That man might have tried to fight you for saying such things to him."

"Ah, whatever, that wouldn't worry me, I could outrun him any day of the week," retorted Jonathan, replete with confidence in his own prowess.

The brightest spot in all of their lives was Rosie. Round little cheeks, curly blonde hair, exuberant energy, enchanting smile, and a sunny disposition combined with an insatiable curiosity had them all enjoying many a hilarious moment.

"Frankly," Suzanne whispered to Jonathan one evening after Rosie had entertained them with an animated, but unintelligible monologue, "I think even your mother laughs at her antics; well . . . that is when no one is looking."

"That's our precious baby girl," Jonathan whispered back, then crooned into Suzanne's ear, "that's my baby," then added, "Ain't she wonderful? I've a gorgeous wife, an adorable daughter, a handsome son . . . what a lucky man I am!"

The moment brought Suzanne to misty longing for those

former joys that seemed now to be so far out of their reach. Baby Johnny cried. Maggie Mae appeared suddenly, frightening Molly who scampered quickly away, taking the momentary illusion of happiness with her.

"What's wrong with your wife? Scared of her own shadow is she?" Maggie Mae asked Danny querulously, at which everyone else hastily cleared the room.

Hours later, Suzanne cried hard into her pillow--quietly, so as not to wake the sleeping household.

CHAPTER NINETEEN

There were days in February when that good old California sunshine reappeared, bringing new strength to Suzanne. Whenever he could, Jonathan took Suzanne, along with the children, to visit their favorite spots in the surrounding meadows and hills.

Once more, they sat side by side among the wild lavender and sage with a picnic lunch as Rosie gamboled about with great abandon amongst the grassy knolls. Baby Johnny would lie placidly near them, rarely demanding attention. He was not as robust as his sister had been, causing Suzanne a great deal of concern.

Oft times, Jonathan would bring along his fishing pole and though Suzanne was not ready to fish again, he would explain to Rosie the finer points of fishing. Though she could not possibly comprehend what he was telling her, it was obvious she adored her father and found much pleasure sitting by his side as he held the fishing pole, patiently waiting for a fish to bite. When one did, her squeals of delight made Suzanne laugh aloud.

Suzanne longed for those carefree days with Jonathan dancing in the moonlight or hiking in the sunshine along the mountain trails, yet she was grateful for these mellow moments together. They brought drastic improvement to her spirits and her health.

Surprisingly, Maggie Mae had left the lace curtains intact at the east bay window affording Suzanne many mornings of pleasure as she sat feeding Johnny while watching the sun rise beyond the San Gabriel Mountains.

And to Suzanne's delight, Molly proved to be a charming companion. She was well read and loved the same movies as Suzanne. Molly also loved perusing magazines for the latest in fashion, bringing Suzanne a renewed sense of excitement about her wardrobe. Molly was a seamstress who knew how to restyle old things to make them look fresh and new. It seemed she could work magic. The 1930's style of feminine draping and sinuous folds showed off the contours of Suzanne's petite yet rounded figure perfectly. Molly promised to make Suzanne a dress for summer designed with the latest rage in necklines, the halter.

Danny had retired from the Navy and was looking for work. There were days when Jonathan and Danny worked and days when they simply looked for work. Other days, the men stayed home, working on various handyman projects around the house, giving Molly and Suzanne lots of time to talk.

Molly had lived in San Francisco for just a few years before marrying Danny. Prior to that, her home had been Ireland, the land of her birth. She often played with little Rosie while Suzanne tended to baby Johnny or helped Maggie Mae prepare dinner. Molly was too frightened of Maggie Mae to venture into the kitchen and Maggie Mae vented her disdain on a regular basis to Suzanne about Molly's ineptness. As such, it seemed the best part of wisdom to keep the two women apart.

Evenings generally found the four of them in the living room, listening to the radio after the children were asleep and Maggie Mae was off in her own world. More often than not, however, Molly entertained them with stories of growing up in Ireland or Danny told of his world travels with the Navy. On the rare Saturday nights when Rosie was with her grandparents, the two couples would sneak out to the new movie palace as baby Johnny slept in contentment on Jonathan's lap.

Suzanne felt that Danny and Maggie helped lighten the gloom surrounding the depressing house and mordant Maggie Mae. She would never grow accustomed to what went on behind that locked hall door; often wondering just how much Molly knew about it all.

For Suzanne, leaving to live in their own place again could not come any too soon, though she hoped when they did, that they would still manage to see Danny and Molly often. When she asked, Jonathan would give a vague, unsatisfactory reply. However, until Suzanne regained her full strength and Jonathan found a decent paying job, their prospects for moving seemed about nil.

Grace would not come near Maggie Mae's house, but encouraged them to bring Rosie and Johnny to visit occasionally.

Living with Maggie Mae made Suzanne feel she had lost the tenuous touch she was just re-establishing with her family, along with a sense of returning to her true self, while living at the cottage. Whenever she thought of it, she felt such incredible despair.

"No matter," she regularly told herself, "we will be back in our own place eventually and I will try again. We will find our blue skies once more!" Jonathan loved her, he was trying hard, she had her wonderful children and, that was all that mattered.

February turned into March bringing with it more rain and gusty winds. Due to the inclement weather, their family adventures had to be curtailed meaning the seven of them were crowded into the house together much more frequently.

Maggie Mae grew ever more sour, venting her anger at whoever happened to be in her way. She obviously doted on Rosie, but commented regularly on that "scrawny baby" who she appeared to dislike intensely. Suzanne never left his side when Maggie Mae was roving about the house for fear his grandmother would startle him. Whenever Jonathan was holding the baby, Maggie Mae glowered in disgust.

Jonathan was growing discouraged about his lack of regular work. He started leaving in the evening after Suzanne was ready for bed, stating that he was "checking on things." This sounded a rather ineffectual excuse; however, Suzanne had little energy left for discussion at such an hour. He would not return until long after Johnny's midnight feeding causing sleep to elude her.

The next day, Jonathan would be edgy and grumpy, smelling strongly of stale beer and cigarettes. Suzanne was dismayed at this turn of events, while Jonathan was strangely adverse to any discussion of the matter.

The effervescent, cocksure, boisterous albeit gentle man she married appeared to be slipping away from her and she was worried.

There was no one, however, with whom she could discuss those fears. During the midnight hours she mulled them over and over in her own mind until at times she thought she would go crazy. At such times, she would turn the radio on softly to the latest songs, tap her feet in rhythm to the music, and dream of their former dancing days. She read, too, burying herself in the lives of the characters, trying to forget her gnawing concerns over Jonathan's change in behavior. When all else failed, she would slip into the kitchen for a glass of homemade wine, or two. It helped, but only for a time.

The morning would come again, bringing back her fears with it.

March, 1931
Glendora, California

CHAPTER TWENTY

It was a blustery, cold day in mid-March. Suzanne woke with a start, followed by a sense of foreboding. Rosie was with her grandparents, Jonathan had not returned to their bed at all during the night, and Johnny had not wakened yet for his early morning feeding.

It was too late, something was wrong.

Suzanne flew across the room to Johnny's crib, fearing he was ill, wondering how she would get him to the doctor if no one was around to drive them. Her mind was in frenzied whirl as she reached her son. She stopped. His skin was an odd ivory color she had never seen before, almost like tallow candle wax. Reaching over to scoop him up, she realized his skin was extremely cold.

In a hollow, piercing voice she shrieked, "He's not breathing."

There was a rushing sound in her ears; then she felt the worn carpet directly beneath her elbow. The room became a swirl of faces as she fell, but it was Jonathan's face that she saw through her terror. It was frozen into a mass of horror and fear. He grabbed the baby from her and shouted in his face, "Breathe, Johnny, breathe. Oh, my baby boy, breathe! Please breathe."

It rapidly became apparent to everyone who had entered the room that Johnny was no longer alive. Jonathan crumpled to the floor beside Suzanne, laid his head down and moaned, "I should have been here. Maybe I could have done something to save him."

The room became absolutely still, no one stirred. Then, Danny took charge.

"The authorities will have to be called immediately as well as the doctor."

Suzanne was not aware that Maggie Mae had a phone in the house. She watched in amazement as Danny strode to his mother's bedroom, forced the door open and yanked a phone from beneath the bed.

"She did not want anyone using it. Said it cost too much and needed to be kept free for her gentleman callers," Jonathan whispered in Suzanne's ear. "Mother has threatened dire consequences if anyone touches that phone."

Suzanne thought she was beyond being shocked by Jonathan's mother, but to her surprise, she was not. Forcing those thoughts from her mind, Suzanne picked up baby Johnny's body and laid it gently on the bed.

Stroking his forehead, she softly sang his favorite lullaby, weeping profusely.

When the police officers arrived, they ordered everyone into the living room for questioning. Dr. Stevens arrived soon after and took charge of the infant body.

Maggie Mae had slipped from the room as the officers entered the front door, and she did not follow everyone into the living room. The officers told everyone to be seated as they asked, "Is everyone present who was in the house at the time the body was discovered?"

Suzanne could only shiver convulsively. Jonathan simply stared at the man. It was Molly that cried out, "She's not here; Danny's mother is not here!"

"She will have to be found and brought in here," the officer in charge told her quietly.

Molly looked aghast. "I have no control over that old hag," she replied, then quickly covered her mouth as she slumped against Danny.

"I will find her, go ahead and ask your questions," Danny said rising from the davenport.

"I need to know, who was the last one to see the baby alive?"

Suzanne spoke up, her voice racked with pain, "Well, I am certain that would be me. He had his last feeding about midnight. He usually wakes for his next feeding at about 4:30 or 5:00. I woke late and realized he had not cried for his bottle, so I rushed to his side and found him . . . saw he was not . . . that he was . . ."

"That's fine, ma'am. We just needed to know."

As the officer was asking them questions, a second officer was searching the bedroom.

"Nothing amiss in there, sergeant. Not that I can see, anyway. Don't know much about babies, but it all looks normal to me."

Maggie Mae glided quietly into the room, sullenly looking up into the sergeant's face.

"What do ya need me for? I don't know nothin' about that baby. It's her concern," she said, pointing a shaking finger at Suzanne.

"Well, ma'am, the law says that we have to question everyone present in the house to determine if there has been foul play."

"Foul play, you say, in this house?" Maggie Mae responded with the oddest smile. "By no means, not in this house," she finished with a derisive laugh. The second officer glanced her way with a knowing look, but the sergeant went on with his questioning.

"Sir, where were you this morning when your wife found the baby?" the sergeant asked Jonathan.

With a start, Jonathan replied, "In the kitchen, getting myself some breakfast. I was about to head out for work when I heard Suzanne scream."

"Once we have the doctor's findings, we will file a report on the matter. I can't say one way or the other what the findings will be. In the meantime, you may prepare for the baby's burial." With that comment, the men left.

It did not seem the day could hold any further shocks, but

Suzanne had not thought of such a thing. They would be putting her baby in the cold ground, away . . . away from them--forever.

"Where is he?" she wondered, not realizing she was speaking aloud. "Is he truly gone?"

Molly reached over and took her hand.

"My Granny said all babies go to heaven. They're too young ta' be sinners yet," Molly said slipping back to her native brogue. "So God lets 'em in the pearly gates, for free so to speak. Me' muther, she had a baby die, and that's what my Granny told her. I think it's true, don't you? Babies are innocent. Surely God lets 'em into heaven, don't you think. Danny, don't you think that's true?"

Danny looked sheepish.

"I don't know, Molly dear. I've never thought of it before. But that sounds good to me. Baby Johnny, being in heaven. That sounds good to me."

Throughout this interchange, Jonathan did not move or even appear to be listening. He simply continued to stare, reflectively through the large, multi-paned window.

"That brings me a lot of comfort, Molly. I am going to believe that Johnny is in heaven with God. I wish, though that I could see him once more . . . just to give him a little kiss, tell him how much I loved him, feel his face against mine, touch his cheeks . . . just one more time." Suzanne groaned softly.

Oh, how she needed Jonathan right now, to hold her; to stop her from shaking. He did not, though. Jonathan did not even appear to even notice as she sat shivering and crying next to him.

The room grew very still once again. Then Suzanne asked in confusion, "Jonathan, what did they mean, about 'foul play' . . . do you think that they think . . . think that one of us did something to Johnny? We all love, I mean loved Johnny, he's our precious baby boy."

"Yes, we all loved Johnny, nobody here would hurt him." Jonathan responded, but his eyes conveyed a puzzling mixture of fear and desperation.

"Jonathan, what did you mean when you said, 'if I had been here maybe I could have saved him?' You were here; here in the house this morning, you said you were."

"I was, Suzanne. But I was not in our room last night," Jonathan said as he put his head in his hands and wept.

Danny walked over to Jonathan, put his hands on his shoulders, and said, "Oh, my dear brother, these things can happen to babies. I've heard of it before. They just die in their sleep, there's nothing to be done for it. Don't blame yourself."

"I just hope that is what the doctor says happened. I just hope . . ." and he wept again.

Suzanne did not know what Jonathan was thinking; he seemed to be avoiding her and her heart was swollen and bleeding from their loss. She felt strangely woozy.

"I believe I will lie down for a bit, rest, get ready for what is ahead," she said as she left the room, hoping Jonathan would follow.

He did not.

Instead, Danny said, "Jonathan let's see what you and I can do about making those burial arrangements."

Suzanne fell on the bed, too spent to cry any more. At that moment she realized that her parents would have to be told and so would Rosie. And she wondered, "How does a mother tell a 15-month old toddler that she will never see her baby brother again?"

Suzanne moaned and curled herself into a ball of abject misery.

"Why? Why did my baby Johnny have to die?

"Why, oh! why, oh! why?"

CHAPTER TWENTY-ONE

The morning was gloomy, the sun hidden somewhere beyond the thick gray clouds. A heavy mist filtered down from the foothills, enveloping the landscape, causing it to be damp and extremely chilly. A nice looking young man dressed in a business suit stood before everyone as they sat huddled around the tiny white casket.

Suzanne was unable to comprehend the finality of this day. Jonathan sat stoically, unmoving. Since the day of Johnny's death, he had not cried again, said it wasn't a man's way--to cry.

Little Rosie, however, was inconsolable.

"Where my baby, mama? I see Johnny now! Where's he go, mama?" Rosie asked again and again. Suzanne tried to explain by saying he was in heaven. Rosie was simply too young to understand. She kept right on asking for her baby "bruver" as a sob would catch in her throat. Her grandmother Stuart stayed home today so she could take care of Rosie. Suzanne did not want little Rosie remembering Johnny lying in that thing, that horrible box.

"On this dismal day filled with sorrows, the Savior invites you to 'Come unto me all you who are weary and find rest for your soul,'" the young man said.

That sounded wonderful to Suzanne, her heart, her spirit, her very soul--it felt like they were bleeding. And, she was weary, oh so weary of struggling, pain, and loss. Finding it hard to really listen, her mind wandered in and out of the scene before her.

"Because I live, you will live also."

What did he mean by that--who is he saying will live, not Johnny. They'd put Johnny in that awful casket and she would never see him again. Suzanne felt woozy. Sobbing she leaned against Jonathan, reaching for his hand. He gripped it so hard, she thought her bones would break, but it felt so much better to have him touching her.

She looked at her father. His head was down and tears were splashing on his best suit.

Her mother was . . . concentrating intently on the man who was speaking. That was puzzling; Grace did not listen much to anyone. Suzanne had asked her mother to find someone to conduct a little service for Johnny. It did not seem right to just stick him in the ground without doing something, saying something. Grace said she found this man she called a preacher at the Methodist church near Grandpa Hughes' bank. It was the church her parents were married in, but Suzanne did not think they had never been there since.

"I guess that is why she is paying such close attention," Suzanne thought. "Or maybe it is because he is so earnest, and good looking." Suzanne caught herself, why was she thinking such thoughts at a time like this.

"I am the resurrection and the life. He who believes in Me, though he may die, he will live. Whoever lives and believes in Me will never die."

"What does he mean, who is he talking about?" Suzanne wondered, not realizing she had spoken out loud.

"Jesus," Molly leaned in from behind her and whispered.

"Oh!" replied Suzanne not really knowing why that man was talking about baby Jesus . . . maybe he meant baby Johnny . . . but, why wouldn't he say so and anyway it didn't make sense talking about baby Johnny like that? It was too much to think about right now so she wouldn't think about it.

Molly making a remark reminded Suzanne about Maggie Mae and her refusal to come to her only grandson's funeral service.

"He was a scrawny, ugly thing. Not beautiful like his father was, didn't deserve to carry the name. Don't care to go see him buried." Maggie Mae told her the day before the service.

That woman never ceased to amaze with her callous, cold-hearted remarks. Suzanne was too stricken to even answer her.

"The Lord is close to the brokenhearted; He rescues those whose spirits are crushed."

"That's me," Suzanne thought as she pondered the preacher's words.

"Jesus said, 'Peace I leave with you, my peace I give unto you: not as the world gives, give I unto you. Let not your heart be troubled, neither let it be afraid.' He's here right now, waiting and wanting to give you His peace."

There was that name Jesus again. Maybe she should find out more. Peace seemed like such an elusive state of mind. Here one day, gone the next with life rushing on, changing when you least expected it to. How could anyone find peace with all the hardships they had experienced lately?

And, their baby, dying--just like that, no warning, no time to say good-bye. That was the part Suzanne could barely grasp. Her baby, dying with no one to hold him, love him, kiss him. That was just tearing her apart, her little Johnny was gone, gone forever and she did not tell him good-bye.

"Weeping remains for a night, but joy comes in the morning."

Joy, happiness, peace--Suzanne was certain she would never feel any of those again. She barely felt alive any more. How could she—her baby was in that casket, and Jonathan was acting so strange and distant, and then there was living again with that woman, with Maggie Mae, it was torturous and she was . . . Ah, but Rosie, she needed to take care of Rosie. She could not allow her darling little girl to see her so dispirited. She had to pull herself together; she had to find a way to be strong, for Rosie.

"Death was swallowed up in victory at the cross. Jesus Christ's triumph over sin and the grave made your salvation possible. Do not grieve as those who have no hope. If you know the Savior, if you have accepted the sacrifice he made for you at

Calvary, you will see Johnny again in Heaven, in Heaven where every tear will be wiped from your eyes. There will be no more death or mourning or crying or pain in Heaven."

That preacher was talking about Heaven. That is where Molly said Johnny went, to Heaven. This man sounded sure of something, like well, oh, she was not sure of what he was saying. Molly said Johnny went to Heaven because he was a baby, an innocent baby. That's what Molly said. Suzanne knew she was not innocent. For one thing, she had deceived her parents and run off to marry Jonathan. Then there was the way she felt about Maggie Mae, hated her almost, and . . . oh, this was just too hard. It hurt too much.

What did that man know anyway? He was so young, probably not even married nor had any children, he could not know about what she and Jonathan were feeling. She was not going to think about this anymore. She had to get strong, toughen up about this thing so she could take care of her little Rosie.

Suzanne looked up to see that they were lowering baby Johnny's casket into the ground. She grew perfectly still. Although it felt like the pain was exploding inside her chest, it was time to stop crying. Johnny was gone, he was dead, there were men putting him down into the ground. Maybe he was in Heaven, she desperately wanted to believe that, but wherever he was, she could not see him or hold him ever again. The thought of it was too painful to bear.

"And so, Lord Jesus, we commit this baby's soul to

Heaven. Please give your peace to this grieving family. Amen."

It was over, it was finally over.

In painful silence, Suzanne watched as they shoveled dirt over the pristine white casket.

"How disgusting," she recoiled in panic, "it is getting all soiled. It will be ugly and then the worms will crawl . . . oh, I cannot think about that anymore." She would stop grieving now for baby Johnny because little Rose needed her. She would not allow herself to feel this horrible pain any more . . . for her girl, Rosie Anne.

She stood and almost fell. Jonathan steadied her. Molly came over and hugged her; then kissing her on the cheek, she said, "That was beautiful, a beautiful way to remember our little Johnny."

Suzanne felt there was nothing beautiful about any of it. She was never going to think about any of this again. She would look forward, not back. She was ready to go and she could tell, so was Jonathan. Her mother, however, was up by the graveside, talking to that man, that man she called a preacher. It looked like there were tears in her mother's eyes. Suzanne was certain she had never seen tears in her mother's eyes. As she watched, her mother lowered her head; and to Suzanne's complete amazement, Grace allowed the preacher to put his hands on her shoulders. Imagine, a stranger touching her mother. The man bowed his head down and seemed to be saying a blessing or something over her mother.

When Grace raised her head, she smiled and her face

looked, radiant. Suzanne had never seen her mother look like this, ever!

Although she wondered what had gotten into her mother, it was time to go. Suzanne just wanted away from this moment, this place, and this day. She wanted to leave, right now.

"Jonathan, let's go get Rosie. I want to leave now."

"Yes, I need my little Rosie, I do. Let's go get our girl."

Almost running, Jonathan and Suzanne fled to the old roadster as Danny and Molly quickly followed behind. Suzanne turned and saw her father, standing by the grave looking completely bereft as her mother continued talking with the preacher. Suzanne's heart was torn apart by the sight of her father in such misery; but she had to go, had to go and reclaim their little Rosie from Grandmother Stuart, right now before the pain enveloped and sunk her.

As they drove away from the graveyard, black clouds dumped a full load of rain onto the roadway, causing it to become almost obliterated. In that instant, gloomy days, filled with rain, became inexorably linked in Suzanne's mind with the pain wrenching her entire being and the hopeless, searing sense of loss haunting her throughout this horrible day.

July, 1931
Glendora, California

CHAPTER TWENTY-TWO

Nothing was stirring in the dead of the night, not even the usual rustling beyond the door down at the end of the hall. Though it was well after midnight, the heat was still oppressive. No mountain breezes played among the trees to cool things off after the scorching summer day.

Nevertheless, luminescent rays from the full moon streamed through the windows, keeping Suzanne from sleep. Normally she enjoyed the loveliness. Tonight, however, she tossed and turned and pondered.

As always, her thoughts centered on Jonathan's perplexing change in behavior and their eroding relationship. In the five months since Johnny died, Jonathan spent most evenings away from home. His occasional beer or two had been replaced by copious amounts of "bathtub gin" imbibed at the local speakeasy. When Suzanne tried to dissuade him, asking if he wouldn't rather stay home, listening to the radio or talking with Molly and Danny, he would shake off her pleas with a disgruntled "no!"

"What is to become of us?" she wondered, mulling

dispiritedly over the events of the past few months. "Although he is still looking for a better paying job, he is so hung over each day, I am sure his state is soon apparent to potential employers. No one will hire such a man."

Danny went along some nights and they would arrive home at a decent hour with Jonathan not so very drunk, though singing lustily at the top of their voices of fishies, lamplighters, and bluebirds. But, Danny wanted to be home with Molly most nights and Suzanne certainly understood why. Besides, Jonathan was not Danny's problem to solve, although he seemed to be trying valiantly to help out.

Right after the funeral, things had not been quite so bad. But now, Jonathan was morose, non-communicative, and oft times harsh with her. He went out drinking and stayed out late. Yet, it was not every night nor was he coming home drunk every time. If she called him on the harshness, he would apologize and things would smooth out for a day or two.

Something had happened, something had changed, and Suzanne had no idea what had gone so wrong. Jonathan would not talk to her about it. All she could figure was that it had something to do with the day she found Johnny's little pillow, apparently thrown to the back of their closet.

She'd said, "Look, Jonathan, it is Johnny's little pillow that Grandmother Stuart embroidered with his name--Jonathan Patrick Kelly, Jr. It has been missing. I have no idea how it got back there. But, I'm so happy to find it!" Suzanne cried a little as she hugged the pillow to her heart.

Jonathan looked startled, almost fearful, and then angry.

"There is panic in his eyes," Suzanne had thought in surprise at the time, as a shiver traveled her spine. It was all behind them now--the investigation, the questions, the suspicions about the cause of the baby's death eventually been ruled a "crib death" by the police department. Was Jonathan involved somehow? She simply could not believe that of him. Yet, it was the look of fear and panic in his eyes which continued to disturb her waking moments.

After that day, he retreated farther away than ever. And, he started leaving every night as soon as Rosie went to sleep.

It was understandable that a married man would feel inadequate living under his mother's roof with no apparent prospects for a steady enough income to move out. However, surely he realized the excessive drinking along with staying out far into the night was not conducive to resolving their problems. Suzanne wished for someone to ask. She had no idea how to reach past the stone wall Jonathan had erected or how to find their way back to even a semblance of their former life.

Fortunately, since Johnny's funeral her mother seemed kinder, gentler somehow. It was a relief to Suzanne; her hands were full with Maggie Mae and now Jonathan's saturnine moods. Suzanne and Rosie were seeing her parents and extended family more often. Jonathan would drop them off to visit while he went job hunting. It helped Suzanne bear the paralyzing grief and discouragement along with her utter dismay about their unraveling life.

It was better to visit Grace without Jonathan present, as her softening personality did not extend in his direction. The rest of the family accepted Jonathan, but Grace did not feel him worthy and she made no attempt to hide her feelings, even for Rosie's sake. Bless Jonathan's heart; he did keep trying to win her mother's good will. As yet, Grace was not aware of her desperate situation with Jonathan; and Suzanne was endeavoring to keep it that way. Grace had no patience for excesses from anyone.

Surprisingly, her mother was going to church every Sunday now and asked if she could take Rosie along sometimes. Suzanne felt it could not hurt. However, Jonathan said, no. He said Sunday was a day for family. Yet, he was often so hung over that there was little joy for Suzanne in spending the day together. His bountiful love for Rosie was the only bright spot on those days as he said little or nothing to Suzanne.

Molly told her to leave Rosie with them and go out with Jonathan at night. Suzanne just could not, Rosie still had terrible nightmares where she called and called for her baby "bruver." Suzanne could not bear the thought of her crying out, only to realize her mother was not there.

Once, Rosie stayed overnight with her parents. Before leaving, Suzanne gave them strict instructions to listen for her cries. She went with Jonathan to the speakeasy where she had a glass of wine and relaxed. Dancing again was exhilarating; it had been so long. As always, dancing with Jonathan was wonderful, like being on clouds. Suzanne felt 17 years old again and alive. Jonathan seemed almost happy.

When Jonathan kissed her passionately in the moonlight, Suzanne was certain they were on their way back to finding skies-of-blue kind of happiness.

However, the moment they pulled up to Maggie Mae's house, Jonathan's melancholy had descended once more.

If not for Rosie, Suzanne was certain she'd slip into an abyss from which she would never return. Her heart hurt all the time. She longed for Jonathan to hold her, to whisper that he loved her, to sing silly songs, to make her laugh again. But, he did not.

The dawn was breaking over the mountains, turning the foothills shades of soft rose and delicate lavender, when Jonathan stumbled into the room.

"Jonathan," Suzanne called out sleepily, "I've missed you so. Won't you come and hold me?"

He was very drunk and did not respond.

"Jonathan, don't you realize how you are hurting yourself and us?" Suzanne could not help but ask. "We need you."

"Oh, just leave me alone, I'm tired."

Something inside Suzanne snapped. He was tired. She was the one trying to keep their lives together, show Rosie only his good side, trying to make sense of it all, enduring life with his mother, living again in poverty . . . and, so she cried out harshly,

"Jonathan that is nonsense. You are the one staying out,

drinking yourself into oblivion, spending time away from us. Maybe even with other women, how am I to know when you do not even talk to me any longer. Are we ever going to move away from here, get a place of our own again? You are tired! Well, I am tired! Tired of living like this! Tired of you being gone, coming home drunk . . . This isn't a marriage, its misery."

There, she'd said it. Told him how she felt. She had kept this all in for so very long, struggling alone with her grief, fears, and pain. Maybe he would realize now what he was doing to her, to them, to Rosie. Maybe he'd act as he ought.

Instead, he slapped her, hard across the face, twice.

"Shut up! I am sick of you demanding things from me. Leave me alone, you are bothering me. I want to go to sleep."

Stunned, angry, and heartsick, Suzanne turned over, knowing she had to do something about this--tomorrow.

CHAPTER TWENTY-THREE

As soon as Jonathan left for his part time job, Suzanne gathered together everything she could think of that they might need in the foreseeable future. No need to bring lots of clothing for herself, she'd left plenty of things behind in her former bedroom. Hurriedly, she stuffed it all into the luggage in which Edward had brought her things to this house. Quickly she wrote a note:

> *Dear Jonathan:*
>
> *I have loved you with all my heart, for better or for worse.*
>
> *When I left everything behind to marry you, it was for the rest of my life.*
>
> *Last night what you did was unthinkable.*
>
> *I am going home to my parents. If you are sober, you can come to see Rosie in a couple of Sundays while my mother is at church. I wish it weren't this way because I really do love you.*
>
> *I know that Rosie will miss you.*
>
> *With love,*
> *Suzanne*

When she heard Maggie Mae taking a shower, Suzanne glided silently into her bedroom to use the forbidden phone.

Hastily, she dialed her father's private number at the bank.

"Daddy, I desperately need your help. I will answer questions later. Please send one of the workers from the groves to pick Rosie and me up at Maggie Mae's house. Have him come as quickly as possible and meet me on the front porch. I will be watching. Please hurry."

"Suzanne, of course, I'll send someone right away. What has happened?"

"Daddy, I have to tell you later, please just hurry! I must go now."

Breathlessly, she ran back to her bedroom and closed the door.

After making certain they were completely ready to leave, Suzanne sat down to think of what else she might need to do. She looked around longingly at the treasures she still had--her books, some pictures, a few trinkets that she'd kept from her high school days, several gifts from Jonathan and of course, a variety of scrapbooks filled with memorabilia. It was too much to take now; maybe she could send her brother, Edward, back for them later.

For right now it was better that she not draw attention to her movements, better if no one saw her, better not to explain anything to anyone. She considered saying good-bye to Molly; she'd been a marvelous sister-in-law and a true friend. Still, not wanting to put Molly in an awkward position, Suzanne decided against it.

Suzanne was waiting on the porch while Rosie chased

butterflies on the lawn. Rosie sensed her nervousness and so she was chattering away with restless energy. Maggie Mae had gone to the market, Danny was working in the backyard, and Molly was nowhere in sight. She had timed things perfectly. Fearing Rosie's clatter would bring Molly around to the front yard at any moment, Suzanne had just called her to come and play quietly on the porch when Ramon arrived. Her father had been wise to send him. As overseer of the groves, he was strong and also a quick thinker.

"Good morning, Miss Suzanne. Your father told me to come and get you here. He said to hurry and make sure you were kept safe. Is everything alright, Miss Suzanne?"

"Oh, Ramon, it is good to see you again," exclaimed Suzanne as she caught him up in a fierce hug. Startled, he looked around and said, "Miss Suzanne, someone might see you doing that, it just doesn't seem right."

"Ramon, I don't care what people think. I am so thankful to see you, so glad you got here so quickly. Here is my luggage; let's go now. I will explain later."

Suzanne regretted not being able to say good-bye to Molly; nevertheless it was best this way, a quiet and seamless escape. It was Maggie Mae she feared above all others. That woman was as unpredictable as a cat in a room full of fidgety children.

Ramon was blissfully quiet as they headed for home. His strong presence and the Packard's power to whisk her out of harm's way helped Suzanne relax a bit. Rosie fell asleep on her lap. She knew she would eventually have to explain to them all;

but for now, she felt relief. Her lack of sleep, months of anxiety, the hasty departure were taking their toll and Suzanne soon fell asleep also.

The much loved groves and glorious gardens were the next sight that she saw. And then, as Ramon pulled the Packard into the driveway, she saw her mother hurrying across the lawn, consternation written all over her face. Then she saw that her father, unexpectedly home from the bank in the middle of the day, was following close behind.

Rosie awoke and cried out, "G'ammie! G'ampapa!!"

CHAPTER TWENTY-FOUR

A delectable breeze fluttered into the garden where Suzanne sat reading, protected from the summer heat by a canopy of trees overhead. The garden was laden with the delicate scent of lemons and oranges from the groves mingled with the redolent fragrance of roses from the gardens. It brought with it so many memories of her years growing up here, enjoying the beauty, but not treasuring it as she was today. So much tranquility could be found in the midst of such loveliness.

Lines learned long ago of a poem written by Louise Driscoll popped into her head:

> *My garden is a pleasant place*
> *Of sun glory and leaf grace.*

Hearing a rustling, she lifted her head and saw her mother coming toward her with Rosie toddling alongside. Suzanne smiled at the sight of Rosie's chubby little legs trying to match the purposeful stride of her grandmother.

"Suzanne, I have given you three days to rest. It is time that we talk about your future."

With a sigh, Suzanne put her book down on the small wicker table and waited. This would be a most difficult conversation, she was certain of it.

"Rosie, my little darling, won't you go play for a bit over there in the grass. Dolly can go too; maybe you can tell her a story about the trees and the flowers."

"I tell her about fishin' with papa. Where's papa, mama? I want to see papa."

Oh dear, this was not going well already. At the mention of Jonathan, Grace scowled. Suzanne thought quickly of a way to distract Rosie. She called Missy, her parent's dog over to play. Rosie immediately ran in glee toward the placid collie, forgetting all about her doll, her father, and everything else for the moment.

"We need to start by finding the right lawyer to begin divorce proceedings. It is a shame it is too late for an annulment, but there is Rosie to consider and she must be protected. You can stay here for now, of course. You need not worry about that yet. But, you will eventually need to consider your financial future for Rosie's sake."

Panic rose in Suzanne's being as her mother went on making plans and talking about decisions that she was not at all prepared to think about as yet. As usual, her mother never stopped to ask her thoughts or opinions about anything. Suzanne wanted to rise and flee somewhere far, far away. She could not, however, there was Rosie to think of and for now, they were completely dependent on the good will of her parents.

Though Grace was different, often talking of "finding her Savior" and speaking more kindly to everyone, she continued to approach things with the same overbearing force as always.

Beyond the fact that she had been going to church every Sunday, several things puzzled Suzanne about her mother lately. For instance, this morning, she found Grace reading from the big family Bible that sat on the mahogany stand in the library. No one ever touched the thing, except maybe to dust it. She was not certain why her mother would want to read from it. And then, there was the fact that her mother appeared to be almost happy, certainly she was smiling more often. Suzanne also observed that there appeared to be less strain between her parents.

"Of course, Rosie should not be around her father. The less she sees of him, the sooner she will forget about him."

About this matter she must take her stand, "No, Rosie will see her father. She adores him and he adores her. He has never once been unkind or harsh with her in any way."

"Nevertheless, he is a criminal. Drinking all night at a speakeasy, those places are illegal! Why, he could be arrested you know."

"Yes, I suppose that is a possibility. But mother, there are lots of people all over the country who frequent their local speakeasy; no one considers them criminals. Anyway, it is the owners of those places who are usually held on charges."

"You never know what might happen . . ." Grace started and then stopped as Suzanne rose hastily and called to Rosie. "We will just have to discuss this at a more convenient time. It seems you are not ready to face up to the facts, as yet anyway. And, let Rosie play with Missy a bit longer," her mother said in that firm voice, "they are having fun, I will watch them."

The tranquility Suzanne had experienced earlier evaporated, leaving her feeling shaken and despondent. She decided a walk in the groves might help.

Ambling along the worn brick path, her straw cloche hat shading her eyes, Suzanne ran smack into her grandfather who was discussing the lemon harvest with Ramon.

"I'll send over those extra workers tomorrow, looks like you'll be needing 'em more than I will, at least for a week or so," Grandpa Stuart said to Ramon in parting.

"Suzanne, you look distressed. What is the matter, dear heart?"

It was all so unexpected that Suzanne burst into tears and threw herself into her grandfather's arms.

Between sobs she blurted out, "Grandpa, why must my mother be so . . . so mean spirited? Just when I think she is becoming more understanding . . . less harsh, she starts in at me again . . . pushing me . . . do you understand her, she's your daughter. I know she is my mother and I . . . Oh! I don't know what I am to do about anything right now."

Grandpa Stuart gently led her away from the workers who were watching curiously to a bench at the side of the packing shed.

"Suzie girl, your mother loves you."

"It doesn't feel like it to me."

"But, she does."

"She certainly has an odd way of showing it."

"I know," Grandpa replied as he took a kerchief out of his pocket and wiped her tears away. "Your mother loves her family . . . very fiercely . . . which . . . well you know, it comes across as harshness sometimes. She is becoming more aware that she's pushed everyone too hard in the past. Your grandmother and I realize that she has often crushed your spirit with her overbearing ways; she is trying to change, she told me so the other day. Believe me; she just wants the best for you Suzanne . . . But, old habits are hard to break, and she is worried about you. And, she is worried about Rosie, too. It is hard for her to see you hurting so. Try to understand that."

"Oh, grandfather, I feel so confused. I love Jonathan, but he's been, he's been awful, so hard to be around, and he hurt me. Rosie needs her father; even if he's not been himself and I'm . . . it's just that . . . oh, I wish . . . ."

"Suzanne, grief's hard to bear, especially when you're young. And, oh you both have such limited experience to meet it with . . . Jonathan has chosen a poor way to manage the loss of his son, yet, I do believe he loves you. Give him time to realize what he has lost . . . Give yourself time to heal. Try to forgive your mother, she means well; she is trying to improve."

"Thank you, Grandpa. I will try. It has been so very nice to be home again, to see you more often. I did not realize how much I have missed being here. I wish my mother would accept Jonathan and that Jonathan would let father help him out."

"Sometimes a man feels he's got to make his own way, Suzie girl."

"You helped dad by giving him these groves."

"It was different somehow. Your dad was already successful, had an established career when he married. This wedding gift was given because . . . well, because . . . your parents married with all of our consent. I know that is hard for you to hear. Nevertheless, it does make things different."

"I know, Grandfather," Suzanne said very quietly.

"Jonathan feels he has to prove himself to us, to your mother. If he takes from them, he will feel as though . . . it's just that he'll feel that they own him. Jonathan's too free spirited for that, it would break him. He is a hard worker, anyone can see that, and these tough economic times will pass . . . besides, well I just believe he'll find his way again."

"Do you really believe that Grandpa?"

"Yes, my darling, I do. Give it some time. And, remember what I said, your mother loves you."

"But not Jonathan . . . you know how she feels about Jonathan. It is almost as like . . ."

"I know that, let's just hope that maybe someday she will see the good in him."

"I hope so, for Rosie's sake."

"Speaking of Rosie, let's go find her. I've a peppermint stick to give her."

CHAPTER TWENTY-FIVE

The Packard glided smoothly along as Suzanne gazed out the window at the passing scenery. Her mind wandered back over the past week and the many changes she had experienced.

Her parents were doing their best to make her feel comfortable and yet, she missed Jonathan. Pondering Grandpa Stuart's words made her realize that Jonathan was still aching over little Johnny's death as badly as she, he just showed it differently. Although she continued to be extremely wounded over Jonathan's behavior, at least she understood him better since her talk with grandfather.

Mother had purchased a darling little bed with primrose pink and white dotted Swiss accessories for Rosie. It was a bed fit for a princess. Suzanne was sharing her spacious former quarters with Rosie who was sleeping in the little dressing room. Fortunately, the night dreams about baby Johnny had ceased. Suzanne was ever so glad to have Rosie out of that dismal atmosphere at Maggie Mae's and felt the oppressive atmosphere had most likely contributed to the nightmares.

Of course, Rosie was thoroughly enjoying all the extra

attention from her grandparents, great-grandparents, aunts, uncles, cousins, and the household staff. There was always someone around to play with her as well as lots of room to run about with Missy. However, she missed her father terribly and asked about him each morning. Suzanne reassured her that he would come and see her sometime soon. Rosie was a happy child who accepted her mother's assurances that she would see her daddy very soon. Suzanne could only hope he would come.

In spite of their kind ministrations, it was obvious her parents were very concerned about her future. Grace, in particular, made comments at regular intervals about the need to secure her safety and interests by hiring a lawyer. She also reminded Suzanne on a daily basis that she had given up so much when she married, and that she was lucky to be with her own kind of people again. Grace saw nothing at all good in Jonathan and never missed a chance to point out his failings. Nevertheless, Suzanne was convinced the Jonathan she fell in love with still lurked somewhere beneath his crusty façade of late.

Deep in her soul, she longed for Jonathan to come begging for forgiveness and requesting a second chance. She was not certain what she would say, yet she did want him to ask.

Suzanne felt conflicted. Life was so much easier at her parent's home--there a household staff to do the work, luxurious surroundings, lovely gardens, and freedom from the constant worry about money.

Yet, while living at home again, she had to deal with all

those restrictions associated with life in their social order. Then there was her mother with her relentless, driving ways. Suzanne longed for the life she had with Jonathan while living in their own little cottage. Back then, they had lived and loved so whimsically-- enjoying each day as it came to them. If only Jonathan would let her parents help them out; though, after her talk with grandpa she understood that better now as well.

"Miss Suzanne, we are here," Ramon said as he pulled up to Bullock's Department Store on Wilshire Boulevard. "I'll just wait right out here 'til you are ready. Your father said you should take all the time you want in there. Now don't you be worrying about me, these bones could use time to just sit and rest. Go along now and enjoy yourself."

Sighing, Suzanne gathered her emerald green silk-banded slouch hat and tapestry clutch along with her little white crochet gloves as she exited the Packard. In spite of her excitement about getting new clothes, Suzanne longed for a companion to share in the fun.

This morning as Cook was clearing the sideboard of their breakfast, father had announced, "Suzanne, you have been cooped up here long enough. Your mother and I know you could probably use some new frocks and things. I have arranged for Ramon to drive you into Los Angeles for a day of shopping. Mother will care for Rosie. We want you to just go and enjoy yourself," he said as he handed her an enormous amount of money.

"Oh, Daddy! I really shouldn't take your money. I'm fine,

really."

"It is a gift, please take it. I want you to spend all of it on the things you need. Nothing for Rosie now, we will take care of her needs later."

Realizing that refusing the money would only wound her father, Suzanne accepted it. After dressing in her pale green crepe dress with the cowl neck, donning a pair of white open-toed pumps, and styling her bobbed hair into a soft wave, Suzanne felt ready to enter the glamorous environs of Bullock's and Desmond's.

Silk stockings, two pairs of enchanting shoes, three dresses in the latest vogue, some underpinnings, a kid leather handbag, and a lovely cambric nightgown edged in Brussels lace--she felt absolutely wanton; but oh, how she loved such fine things. Weighed down with packages and heading for the elevator, Suzanne spied Louise, her best friend of long ago. Debating whether to speak, wondering if she would remember, Suzanne realized Louise had spotted her.

"If this isn't the cat's meow, it's Suzanne! Goodness my, you look divine. That dress accents your gorgeous green eyes and sumptuous auburn hair. You always had the grandest sense of style! How have you been? I have not seen you at any of the social events for ages. What have you been doing with yourself? Oh, it's good to see you!" Louise giggled, hugging Suzanne and continuing to talk.

"I was just going up to the salon. I hear Madeleine Vionnet

has a new line out and I want to get an evening dress designed by Madame Grès. Come up with me--you are going to the soiree at the Moore's estate aren't you? Let's go see a movie together sometime. I hear *The Front Page* is just swell."

Overwhelmed, Suzanne did not know how to respond. Apparently, Louise knew nothing of the twists and turns her life had taken, expecting she could jump right into the swing of social events with her.

Suddenly, the enormity of her sudden shift from poverty, grief, and solitude to abundance, gaiety, and glitz took its toll. Suzanne's eyes sprung uncontrollable wells of tears.

"My dearest friend, what is the matter?" Louise queried, looking chagrined. "I am not quite certain what I have said to make you cry. Shall we go find a quiet spot to talk?"

Louise led her to the ladies lounge and helped deposit her purchases on the striped silk sofa. She retrieved a warm cloth from the attendant, pressed it to Suzanne's forehead, and wiped her tears.

Talking soothingly Louise asked, "What has happened? You don't seem yourself at all, is everything going all right for you?"

Not sure where to begin, Suzanne simply responded, "I am married, did you know?"

"I thought maybe . . . I had heard that, but I wasn't sure if it was true, especially when I saw you shopping by yourself and all. I heard you married . . . married someone your parents did not approve of, but I didn't know who it was or where you went to live."

Taking a deep breath, Suzanne went on, "I have a little girl and her name is Rose Anne. We had a son, Jonathan, Jr. He passed away a few months ago. Crib death, they called it. It was so very painful and I am just now starting to feel better."

"You poor dear, how that must have hurt . . . and, two babies already, oh my! But, oh how wonderful. I want a baby some day . . . soon, I hope. I have to get married first, of course. My parents want me to marry Ralph Moore, that's why I want the perfect dress for the soiree. I don't know, he's really not my type, but you know the Moores are simply loaded with moolah, we'd always have plenty. Oh dear, I am rattling on when my best friend from high school is grieving, I am sorry! Are you okay now?"

Realizing that Louise could not really understand all that she had experienced, Suzanne finished by saying, "I am staying with my parents just now. Mother is watching Rosie for me and daddy sent me off to shop today. I need to go; Ramon is waiting for me at the car. I'll be at my parent's for awhile. Call me. Enjoy yourself in the salon," Suzanne said as she gathered her things to leave.

"Oh, you always were such a strong one. Come give me a hug. It's been just nifty to see you again. I'd love to meet your little Rose Anne. Let's get together soon."

After Louise left, Suzanne made her way to the Packard and Ramon. It was hard to believe she had once been that carefree and unfettered. Although she had not yet been to Desmond's and still had some money left, she was exhausted and ready to go home. She could shop another day in Pasadena or at home in Glendora.

Riding back along the familiar roads, she dozed off and dreamed. Jonathan was being himself again, they were happy and carefree. She heard singing, songs they'd danced to, songs like *I Can't Believe That You're In Love With Me, I Wanna Be Loved By You* . . .

She woke with such joy, only to realize it was the radio; she was riding in the Packard and Ramon was turning down the lane where her parents lived.

CHAPTER TWENTY-SIX

"I was hoping you would go to church with me today," her mother said, as Suzanne sat drinking her morning cup of Earl Grey tea in the parlor.

"I will sometime, but I am just not ready for it yet," replied Suzanne carefully as she did not want to upset her mother.

"Maybe Rosie can come with me then."

"Another time, perhaps, I want her to stay with me today. I am planning to sit in the garden and read. I've just started *Shadows on the Rock* by Willa Cather. I thought I would let Rosie play with the new Raggedy Ann and Andy dolls that you bought her yesterday. She is enchanted with them." Suzanne replied, wishing her mother would not get upset, but she did.

"Well, I certainly hope you let her go sometime, the child certainly needs the security that church can afford, what with your uncertain future and all," Grace said as she walked away in a huff.

Then turning back said softly,

"I am sorry, Suzanne. I realize you want time alone with her and she is rather young still. Please, though, will you let me take her sometime? I would really like to do that."

Amazed at her mother's rapid change of heart, Suzanne quickly replied, "Of course, we will all go together next week."

She was hoping that while Grace was not on the premises Jonathan would come to see Rosie today. Suzanne was relieved when her mother finally left for church along with her grandparents.

However, she was concerned that her father had not joined them. No matter, if Jonathan came her father could be handled more easily than her mother.

Ever since Jonathan had helped with the harvest, her father seemed to have more respect for him. She heard Grandpa Stuart tell her father how very hard Jonathan had worked and knew that was the reason.

Rosie played until she grew tired of her dolls.

"Mama, I see papa, I love papa. I want papa play wit' me."

"Rosie, dearest, we will see him soon."

"I see papa, I want see papa now!" Rosie insisted, starting to wail.

Feeling helpless, Suzanne set the book down and cradled Rosie in her arms. Soothing back Rosie's blond curls, she kissed her forehead and said, "Little darling, your papa loves you too. He is just very busy right now; I think we will see him sometime soon. How would you like to go inside and find your grandpapa? I imagine he will play a game of hide and seek with you. Would you like to do that?"

Rosie adored playing hide and seek, especially with her

grandpapa. He always found such comical places to hide that Rosie would laugh and laugh. Suzanne didn't ever remember a time when her father played hide and seek or any other such game with, but she was overjoyed to see him playing so charmingly with Rosie.

"Yes, mama, I play wif' G'ampapa," Rosie replied as she stuck her thumb in her mouth and trotted off toward the house.

Jonathan, however, never came.

Sunday afternoon dinner was the usual boisterous get together with both sets of grandparents along with her father's brother, Walter. Her mother's four brothers as well as their wives and families joined in for the traditional meal of fried chicken, mashed potatoes, fresh corn on the cob, and juicy sliced tomatoes from the garden. Of course, there were several of Grandmother Hughes' pies for dessert--rhubarb, lemon meringue, and chiffon pie.

Suzanne wished for a slice of her Grandmother Stuart's black walnut pie, but the walnuts were not ready to harvest as yet. Grandpa Stuart also hand squeezed hundreds of lemons from the groves for his famous thirst quenching lemonade.

In spite of her sorrow about Jonathan, Suzanne savored this tradition of family gathered round every Sunday afternoon. On this splendid, albeit very warm summer day, she was enjoying wearing one of her new dresses, a navy polished cotton polka dot halter along with her new white strap sandals. Her bachelor uncle, Walter, shyly told her how beautiful she looked. It felt good.

Later in the afternoon, Grandpa Stuart found her curled up in the parlor, reading while Rosie took her nap.

"Suzie, my girl, you looked especially sad today. What's troubling you?" he asked, with his voice booming. Suzanne hoped the whole family could not hear him asking what was wrong as she really did not want to talk about it. Except, well, she really did not mind talking to her grandpa, he seemed to understand.

"Oh, grandfather, you are so dear to notice! I thought Jonathan would come to see Rosie today. She cries for him every day. He knows mother goes to church on Sunday mornings and I was certain that he would come. He didn't." Suzanne replied, her shoulders drooping.

"Dear heart, he's embarrassed. He knows he's done wrong, and . . . well, I think that he simply doesn't know what to say or do right now."

"Why doesn't he just come and tell me he is sorry, then. Surely he misses Rosie. I hope he misses me too . . . He used to tell me no room was the same without me in it. He said and did lots of things that made me feel loved. He told me how pretty I was and, he does love me Grandfather. He made me so happy before this horrible depression took his job and death took our Johnny."

"I know . . . Jonathan's made some very poor choices. Yet, it's hard on a man . . . when he can't find work . . . and feels helpless about it. It is also hard on a man to admit that he's wrong, even when he knows he should. He's afraid, you know, afraid you'll laugh in his face, afraid you don't love him any longer, and well, . . . he feels you shouldn't . . . uh, that is not after what he's done."

"No, I don't know what he's thinking. I do still love him, grandpa. I have been mulling it all over a lot these past few days and I do. Mother keeps telling me to find a lawyer and start divorce proceedings. But, I don't really want to do that. I want Jonathan to come find me here and tell me he loves me and that he cannot stand to live without me and swing Rosie around and smile and make me feel cherished . . . and I want him to say he's going to change and stop acting so distant and frightful."

"Well, then stand your ground! Don't let Grace talk you into doing something you don't want to do . . . just don't let her force you into a hasty decision. You know, we've loved having you around here. . . seeing Rosie so much. It's been grand coming out here, finding you enjoying the beauty of the gardens, walking among the groves, and . . ."

"And, grandpa I've loved being here," Suzanne interrupted. "I didn't realize what a wonderful home I had before I left it, before I lived at Maggie Mae's. Oh, that woman, she is just horrible. I think some of Jonathan's bad behavior is because of her."

"Could be. He's a man now though, needs to own up to his problems, and solve 'em! You know . . . if you truly love Jonathan, give him time . . . time to realize his errors. And, I . . . I do believe that he will. Sometimes life forces people to see things more clearly, and oh, sometimes it's a heart of love, and . . . sometimes both. Give him more time, Suzie girl, and . . . in the meantime, you rest, get refreshed and, then you'll be ready for the next part of life with him."

Suzanne was not certain if she truly believed what Grandpa was saying about Jonathan seeing the error of his ways. It seemed to her that if he had, he would have come already, come to see her and his darling Rosie. She did believe the other things grandfather said, after all he was a man and he understood how men thought. And, she was relieved he told her not to let mother push her into a divorce; it helped to know that Grandpa Stuart was on her side.

"Thank you, grandfather. I have needed you to help me understand. Please, though, don't tell anyone what we talked about; I'm just not ready to talk about it to anyone else. I don't feel strong enough yet to 'stand my ground' as you say. I need more time. Please, don't even tell Grandma, she might tell mother. Promise me!"

"I promise dear heart."

Just then several of her cousins piled into the room.

"We're going to see Charlie Chaplin in *City Lights* over at the Movie Palace on Grand Avenue. Come, go with us Suzanne."

On a whim, she decided to go with them, so went to find her mother and ask if she would watch Rosie. As she went up the stairs, she could see Grandpa Stuart looking up at her, smiling, and she thought, "I think this is what he means I should do, have some fun. It'll be grand to go see a movie again. I have not been to one in a long, long time."

CHAPTER TWENTY-SEVEN

When Sunday came round again, Suzanne was ready to attend church with her mother. For Rosie, she chose a cherry red polka dot dress with the white ruffled pinafore and bouffant petticoat along with her frilly white socks and kid-leather shoes, gifts from her grandparents. For herself, she decided on the white silk georgette dress with fluttering cap sleeves she had purchased with her father's money.

This was a day to please her mother. Even her father seemed to think so as he joined them in the Packard. Having her daughter and granddaughter dressed beautifully in white would do just that and besides, they would stay nice and cool.

The week had passed uneventfully with no word or visit from Jonathan. Suzanne took Rosie to visit Mary and Harvey who were overjoyed to see them. They had not seen Rosie since Jonathan hastily moved them all from the cottage. They were unaware that baby Johnny had died. Although Suzanne had no regrets about her visit to the dear old couple, the trip was a painful reminder of all that had been lost.

Curious, Suzanne scanned the people gathered for worship

at her mother's church. They did not look like the somber, dour people she expected; most of them were smiling. The word she thought to describe them was peaceful. When the music started, Suzanne was incredulous that her mother was joining in the lusty singing. She could not imagine what had come over her mother. Her father stood, but did not sing.

Covertly, she looked at the men in the crowd, so many were singing joyfully. Jonathan loved to sing to her at home. However, she could not imagine him joining in with a crowd like this. Her mother's whole countenance changed as she sang; she actually looked content.

When the preacher rose to speak, Suzanne was certain she would be bored. Yet, she was not.

He talked in such an interesting way about having faith in God. He said that all you needed to have was faith the size of a mustard seed. Suzanne knew about seeds from the groves and Jonathan's gardens. She'd never seen a mustard seed, but it seemed like a really small amount. The point he made, was that when you reached out to God with just a little tiny bit of belief, God could move the mountains.

Suzanne wasn't sure what he meant by that, but she knew a mountain stood between her and Jonathan. She started thinking about that night when Jonathan had been so very mean and had slapped her. From a distance, she heard the preacher saying that if someone has hurt you, it is important to forgive them. She was not certain if she wanted to forgive Jonathan, his behavior had been appalling.

Suzanne tuned back in – just in time to hear,

"If you forgive other people for their wrongdoings, God can forgive your wrongdoings. Now, folks, we've all done things wrong. We've hurt people with our words, we've let them down with our actions, we've thought ill of them in our minds. God says that if we do not forgive others when they fail us, He cannot forgive us when we fail Him."

"Well, I know that I have not been perfect," Suzanne mused, "and I've certainly let my parents down. I hate Maggie Mae, I do. I have been so angry at Jonathan. I've wanted to hurt him back. I guess that I have done some wrong things, but still, I can't just think that what he's done to me is okay. We can't keep on living as we were."

The preacher was still talking. She was not certain she wanted to listen any more until she heard him say,

"Forgiving someone does not mean that you are saying that what they did was acceptable."

Suzanne thought to herself, "Well, that is a better way to think."

"Forgiving someone does not mean that you have to continue a close relationship with them, especially if they do not chose to change their behavior. It simply means that you are not constantly dwelling on what they did to you. It means that you realize each of us have times in our lives when we make wrong decisions or bad choices."

"Ahhh, that is the point," she realized, "I want Jonathan to tell me he is going to change. Grandpa has helped me understand that Jonathan is drinking so much because of his hurt over baby Johnny as well as his frustrations over money and his job situation. Maybe if we could talk to each other about it, I could help him see that and then he would change."

The preacher continued, "It also means that you keep on loving them just like God loves you."

"I do know I love Jonathan."

"Beloved, you must realize, however, that forgiveness can only happen when God's Spirit moves in our hearts and removes the anger and bitterness, replacing it with His goodness and love."

That is where he lost Suzanne. She had no idea what he meant, but she knew there were many things he said that she wanted to think about.

It was over. Suzanne was so lost in thought about what she had heard that she almost did not see her old friend, Tom and his wife, Cassandra talking to the preacher at the door.

"What are they doing here?" she wondered. Tom had never told her he went to church. Once they finished talking, Suzanne positioned herself so Tom would see her standing with Rosie in her arms. She preferred he acknowledge her first, and he did.

"Suzanne, what a delight, I had no idea you came here to church."

"I have never been here before. My mother attends the services here and asked me to come today. It was nice."

"We just started about three months ago. Our neighbors invited us and we came. We . . . we . . . well, we became Christians and we love coming here. We are thinking of joining. Has your mother been coming here for very long? I did not know she was a Christian."

"Is that what it's called?" Suzanne replied. "She's talked about 'accepting Christ as her Savior', but I've never really been sure what that is all about. She started coming here after . . . um, after the . . . um, maybe you don't know," Suzanne started to falter, realizing she felt faint though she was not sure why. It was probably the heat.

"Are you okay, Suzie? You look very pale," Cassandra said as she stepped forward to place her arm securely along Suzanne's back. "You were starting to say . . ."

In a very low, pain filled voice, Suzanne continued, "It was after our baby Johnny died that she started to come. Something happened to her the day of the funeral. She's been different and she started coming here, to church."

Cassandra and Tom drew closer as Cassandra gave Suzanne a gentle squeeze. They glanced at each other, and then Tom said, "Cassandra had a miscarriage a few months ago. It is painful, isn't it? That is when we got to know our neighbors. She is a nurse and came over to help Cassandra on the day it happened. They invited us here. We have found such peace."

Suzanne felt drawn to them and to the peace she felt in this church, yet she felt like running away . . . to a more familiar place.

Her father walked up and gave Tom a hearty handshake. Then he glanced at Suzanne and apparently saw how pale she was.

"I'm afraid we better get our Suzie girl home, out of this heat, and Rosie is restless. Good to see you Tom and Cassandra, is it? I hope we see you again real soon. Drop by the house sometime."

She noticed her father stop and talk to the Sheriff as they left. Here was another surprise, to see the Sheriff at church.

It was a delightful afternoon, with the family all gathered for dinner and afterwards, laying down with Rosie for a nap. It all kept Suzanne busy until early evening. She was giving Rosie a snack when her father appeared, "I need to speak with you as soon as possible, Suzanne."

A chill of apprehension ran up Suzanne's spine at her father's tone of voice. It was not exactly harsh, he never was, however it was stern and somber.

"Certainly, father, let me finish here with Rosie and find someone to watch her."

After washing Rosie's face and hands, Suzanne found Grandmother Stuart sitting in the garden, knitting. Rosie was more than happy to play with Missy while her great-grandmother kept an eye on her.

Meeting her father in the entry hall, she took one look at his face and her stomach started to churn in fear. As they sat down together on the settee in the parlor, her father said, "My dearest, I'm afraid something has happened with Jonathan."

CHAPTER TWENTY-EIGHT

Suzanne sat absolutely still waiting for her father to continue.

"I am sorry to have to tell you that Jonathan was arrested last night. He was at the speakeasy over on Route 66. It was raided. He was taken to the local jail and released this morning. Only the two owners and bartender were held over for a preliminary hearing."

"That is just what mother said might happen. I didn't really think it would."

"Well, Sheriff Donner said the feds have been routing out the smaller speakeasies lately. Previously they have left them alone because of bigger situations to deal with, but now they are cracking down. The Sheriff did not mention anything further about Jonathan, just thought we ought to know."

All Suzanne could think about, for the moment, was that her mother had another reason now to dislike Jonathan.

"Father, what do you think I should do? After that sermon we heard today, I have been thinking about trying to talk to

Jonathan, maybe try to work things out together, see if he won't ask for my forgiveness. I am certain he misses Rosie."

"I need to think about it for a bit, my dearest. It seems the incident may have brought Jonathan to his senses; however, we do not want to rush into things. We have to think of Rosie's well being and about yours as well."

When the door knocker sounded, Suzanne was listening to her father and paid little attention as the maid answered the door. Hearing footsteps, Suzanne looked up just as Jonathan entered the room with a dainty bouquet of lavender primroses surrounded by pale blue forget-me-nots, tied with a creamy white ribbon. Her heart raced; he was so good looking. How she loved that engaging smile of his. As soon as he saw Suzanne, Jonathan bent down on his knees and held out the bouquet to her.

"The flower lady said that in the language of flowers, the primroses mean I cannot live without you and the forget-me-nots that my love for you is true. I am here to beg for your forgiveness," he said in a voice strangled by sorrow. "I have missed you more than I could ever say . . . you and Rosie are my life. Every day has been dreadfully hollow and completely miserable without you."

Thinking quickly, Suzanne motioned for her father to leave the room. She whispered as he walked by, "Please don't tell Rosie he's here. I need to think about what I want to do. I am not ready for her to see him yet when he isn't going to stay and play with her."

And then to Jonathan, as she took the bouquet with uncertainty, "Hello. Thank you for the flowers and taking the time to pick out such a meaningful gift," she said stalling for time to get used to the idea of his apparent contriteness . . . Rosie has missed you terribly and asks about you every day. Let's sit down over here."

He came toward her as if to kiss her. The hastiness of his actions made her rather angry; he had not even acknowledged his atrocious behavior yet.

"I am not ready for that yet, Jonathan. We need to talk first."

"Okay. I guess you are right, but I've missed kissing you, holding you and . . . and . . . all that . . ." he stuttered rather desperately.

"It's nice to hear that you missed me," Suzanne interrupted before he went any further. "However, you hit me Jonathan. Besides that, for the past few months you have been harsh, moody, uncommunicative, and gone from home almost every night, coming in very late drunk or almost drunk. You cannot expect to just come here, even with a request for forgiveness, and expect everything to just be okay again between us." Suzanne said testily.

"I know, Suzanne, you are right. Something happened that made me wake up and realize how wrong I have been."

"My father was just telling me that you have been arrested last night. Sheriff Donner told him this morning. Is that what made you wake up to things?"

"Yes, and Danny. He's been talking to me, telling me I needed to straighten myself up. He reminds me every day what a wonderful woman you are and how lucky I am to have you and Rosie. Danny's been pretty disgusted with me. Told me I don't deserve you, told me I've been a fool and some other things I won't repeat to you. I guess I've deserved that."

"You guess?" she answered him, astonished.

"I know that I do."

At that, she softened a bit, "Jonathan, I love you and I have been thinking of how I could talk to you about things. But, you must know, hitting me is not acceptable at any time! And, there's Rosie, what if you hit her? You must realize my parents are furious with you, especially my mother and they are determined to protect Rosie. My mother has been urging me to get a lawyer and start divorce proceedings."

Jonathan turned quite pale as she spoke.

"I . . . I . . . I know, I don't deserve another chance. I was hoping . . . I meant to say right off how wrong I have been. I would never hurt Rosie, I love her; I've missed her so."

"Of course you have, I know that you love her."

"Honey, won't you come and go to a dance with me. There's going to be a swanky one in Pasadena, this Saturday night. They're having a nifty band and a live singer, too. You could get all dolled up. Come and go dancing with me. Remember, the times we danced in the moonlight, you were always so beautiful and . . ."

Suzanne weakened momentarily thinking about the enchantment in their past, then caught herself.

"It's not time for that yet, Jonathan. You need to show me you have changed. How about if we take Rosie somewhere together? She's been asking to see you every day. Let's meet downtown at the drugstore on Saturday afternoon. We can get some ice cream, then we'll go the park and you can play with her, she'd like that. We can talk some more then. I'm tired just now and ready for you to go."

Jonathan looked surprised. He seemed to think they could just pick up where they left off. The audacity of it made her feel extremely upset; she was quite frustrated by his lack of understanding.

"Alright, I'll meet you in front of the drugstore at 1:00 on Saturday," he said rather dispiritedly. "Also wanted to tell you that Danny and Molly are going to have a baby."

"Oh, Jonathan, that is wonderful. Molly's wanted a baby for so long. Please tell her how happy I am for her. Babies are wonderful aren't they, Jonathan? Remember when you told me that babies are a gift from God. Rosie has certainly been that to us, hasn't she?"

Apparently surmising that Suzanne was relenting, Jonathan softly began crooning their favorite song *Stardust* by Hoagy Carmichael to her. Then he switched to one she didn't really know about remembering the times they'd said "I love you" to each other.

She interrupted him, "I do remember, Jonathan. You need to remember how to behave as a husband and father should. That is what we need to talk about. I will see you on Saturday," Suzanne said as she purposefully walked toward the front door.

She was relieved when Jonathan left without further ado.

Collapsing into her father's fireside chair, she worked at pulling herself together so Rosie would not sense her agitation and confusion.

She was feeling just about ready to face everyone when her mother came briskly into the room.

"You should be ready to take over with Rosie now, Suzanne. Your grandmother is getting tired and Rosie is sleepy. Where is your father? I thought he was in here talking to you. Where did those flowers come from?" she added stridently.

She'd forgotten about Jonathan's bouquet. Hastily she contemplated what to say, and then decided the truth was best. "Jonathan brought them for me. He got on his knees and apologized. We talked a bit, and then decided we'd meet downtown next Saturday so Rosie could see him. He's left and I was mulling things over."

"Well, can you imagine that, he waltzes in here thinking he can just say he is sorry and all is well," Grace said with indignation.

"Mother, didn't the preacher tell us today that we need to forgive others so God can forgive us?" Suzanne asked--her voice mingled with defiance and bewilderment.

Very humbly her mother replied, "Yes, he did, Suzanne. I am afraid it is going to take the power of God for me to forgive Jonathan. You are right; I need to ask God's help on this."

Surprised once again at the changes happening to her mother, Suzanne went over and gave her a mother a kiss on the cheek.

Rosie was dancing up and down the front hall singing with abandon--"Yes, Jesus loves me, Yes, Jesus loves me . . . Yes, Jesus loves me . . . Yes, Jesus loves me" all the while clapping her hands joyfully.

"Oh, that child brings more merriment to this household than we've ever had before," her mother said laughing. "Rosie, come give grandmamma a good night kiss."

"Oh, and Suzanne, I almost forgot to tell you," her mother said as she bent over for Rosie's kiss. "Grandpa Hughes has arranged for us all to go to the Mission Inn in Riverside next Saturday night. Uncle Walter is going to make his professional debut there--playing the piano. What exciting entertainment! Imagine, Walter playing every weekend at such a glamorous spot. We will have to see if Grandma Stuart can watch Rosie."

"Yes, mother, that will be lots of fun," Suzanne replied, thankful the subject had shifted away from discussing Jonathan. "If Grandmother cannot watch Rosie, I am certain my friends, Harvey and Mary will do it."

Although her mother frowned at this suggestion, she stopped just short of complaining about it.

"Come dearest, let's take your bath, then mama will read you a story," Suzanne said, playfully scooping Rosie into her arms.

CHAPTER TWENTY-NINE

Although the dawn was still clinging to the hills, it was obviously going to be another unbearably hot day. Suzanne reclined on the gilded ivory silk chaise lounge that had once belonged to her English great-grandmother. She was still wearing her light cambric nightgown, the one edged with Brussels lace purchased during her shopping excursion in Los Angeles. The slight breeze wafting through the French doors soothed her, though her thoughts were extremely turbulent.

She was afraid of the coming day and so she pondered-- "What if Jonathan did not come to meet them at the drugstore as planned? What if he swept her along with his charms? What did she really feel about Jonathan and her life with him? Did she want to leave the security and luxury of her parent's home in the hope of finding their blue skies once more? What was best for Rosie, for her, and even for Jonathan?"

After stretching and walking around her bedroom a bit, Suzanne continued her musings--"Maybe they really didn't belong together as her mother constantly asserted. Maybe Jonathan would be better off finding someone else more like him, someone that lived more like his family. Maybe Rosie would have a brighter future here in the loving embrace of her extended family." On and on these sentiments rolled in her brain, swirling around her like gusts of wind on a blustery day.

Grateful that Rosie was not awake, Suzanne tried in vain to gather her chaotic feelings into some semblance of order.

Hearing the household stirring, Suzanne realized Rosie would soon be up, prattling with gusto. She rose to meet the day. Better to be bathed and dressed than scattered and ill-prepared. She would have to take things as they came, surely the right answers would soon become clear.

Wanting to hear Jonathan tell her that she was beautiful, Suzanne chose her clothing carefully. After much ado, she finally decided on a dusky rose cotton dress with gauzy flutter sleeves, full skirt cinched by a soft white leather belt, and pale pink chiffon ruffles which went round the neck and cascaded down the front to the white pearl buttons. It was feminine and rather daring at the neckline. It showed off her figure perfectly. She wore a light pink straw hat circled by a band of white silk roses and ribbons that she tied in a big bow at the side of her face. Jonathan liked seeing her in things that brought a "glow" to her "gorgeous" green eyes.

Rosie wanted to wear a simple sun suit that tied at her shoulders along with her red cowboy boots, of course. She rarely wanted to wear anything else. Suzanne rued the day she ever let her wear those silly boots her brother, Edward bought for Rosie so long ago. Today, however, was not the time to fuss over Rosie's footwear; there were more important things to manage.

She had arranged to drive Edward's Model A sports coupe that was left sitting in the garage when he decided to join the U.S. Army Air Corps. Edward rarely wrote. When he did, his letters were almost solely about the various aircraft he was learning to fly. He seemed to be in his element and she was happy for him.

Suzanne grew restless waiting and finally decided to leave early. She still had some of her father's money along with money her mother had given her for Rosie's necessities. Suzanne simply told Rosie they were going to get ice cream. She did not want her disappointed if Jonathan did not come. Rosie might not enjoy shopping, but she would be good in order to have the promised ice cream. She would be ecstatic when she saw Jonathan and all else would be forgotten.

By the time they were to meet Jonathan, Suzanne was certain of several things. She loved Jonathan; he'd brought her spirit release from her mother's constant reminders about "proper decorum." Yet she was not going to just fall into his arms. Courting her would be good for him. Also, they needed to talk about the things that had happened, not just pretend they did not.

Furthermore, she never wanted to visit that horrible house at the end of Lone Hill Road or ever live there with his mother again. She would not sleep in that bedroom where her baby had died and Jonathan had disappointed her so.

And, Rosie was going to grow up in the midst of her extended family. Her mother and Jonathan would have to find a way to get along or learn to stay out of each other's way.

As she walked along with Rosie, heading for the drugstore, Rosie spotted Jonathan and ran to him with a squeal of delighted rapture. He scooped her up in his arms and told her how he'd missed her.

"I loves you dear papa," Rosie said stroking his cheek, and then laying her head on his shoulder.

"Hello, Suzanne. You look ravishing!" Jonathan commented as he looked longingly into her eyes and then his eyes swept her entire frame. He moved to embrace her along with Rosie, but apparently thought better of it and simply kissed her on the cheek.

"Hello, Jonathan. I am happy to see you here."

"I wouldn't miss a chance to see the two most beautiful girls in the world, now would I?" he responded nuzzling Rosie's blonde curls.

Suzanne smiled pleasantly and said, "Rosie has been a good girl while I took care of some shopping. I think she is ready for some ice cream."

"Yes!" Rosie shouted. "Me's ready for ice cream."

The three sat at the drugstore counter savoring their ice cream; so refreshing after being out in the summer heat. Rosie sat between them and chattered to Jonathan about her varied adventures with Missy the dog, her dolls, her cousins, and her new toys. Jonathan listened intently, but his eyes often wandered over to gaze at Suzanne.

They finished and Jonathan asked, "Now, little Miss Rose Anne Kelly, would you like to go play at the park with your papa and mama?"

Rosie jumped up and down with abandon shouting, "Yes, yes, I go play with papa at park!"

Walking slowly, Suzanne and Jonathan became lost in conversation while Rosie trailed a bit behind them. Suddenly they noticed that several people walking toward them were giggling and gesturing. In tandem, Jonathan and Suzanne turned to see that Rosie had removed her sun suit and was walking along wearing nothing but her cowboy boots. She was twirling the sun suit and gaily singing aloud. Suzanne and Jonathan looked at each other and burst into laughter.

Quickly, Suzanne pulled Rosie into her arms.

"Little darling, you must put your clothes back on."

"But, I'm hot," Rosie replied as her bottom lip settled into a pout.

"So is mama, but we can't just take our clothes off and walk around naked in public. Be a good girl and let mama put your clothes back on."

Jonathan's sapphire eyes were twinkling and his grin was wider than usual. Suzanne's shoulders were shaking as she attempted to control herself.

"Oh, how good it felt to laugh together again!" Suzanne thought as they continued on to the park with Rosie, fully clothed, and firmly nestled in her father's arms.

CHAPTER THIRTY

After Jonathan left, Suzanne quickly dressed for their evening at the Mission Inn. She decided on her pale pink silk chiffon dress with the iridescent beaded fringe that covered the bodice, in the long lean "flapper" style that clung to her figure until it flared out just above her knees. She had a matching chiffon cloche hat covered with iridescent beading along with a jaunty pink feather that curved across the left ear over onto her forehead and several pale pink silk roses holding silver dangling beads at the right ear. Just a touch of her auburn hair peaked out beneath the back of the hat. Silvery grey brocade pointy-toed shoes with pearl buttons closures, pale pink silk stockings, and a silver beaded clutch added just the right touch. She felt absolutely divine in her stunning attire!

As the Packard whisked them toward Riverside, Suzanne could not help but miss Jonathan. It was fun to be with her parents and grandparents, yet she missed Jonathan ever so much.

Suzanne was captivated with the breathtaking grandeur of the charming old-world Inn. Her grandmother Hughes could not stop exclaiming to grandfather about the exotic tropical plants and exquisite vibrant flowers that adorned the opulent property. Her parents were enthralled with the soaring domes and towers-- architecture so reminiscent of a European castle.

Strolling along the captivating arched walkway, softly awash in golden light from Spanish lanterns hanging overhead, Suzanne caught a glimpse of the night sky shimmering beyond the portico and smiled. How often she had gazed with Jonathan at boundless glimmering stars chasing each other round a luminescent moon, what lovely memories the scene stirred.

The Lounge, nearly filled to capacity, was difficult to navigate as they entered from the sumptuous Rotunda. Fortunately, Uncle Walter had reserved a table for them near the piano. He rose to meet them, his face aglow with anticipation, his body tense with a bit of stage fright. After all, it was a rare privilege to perform at the world famous Mission Inn before such an illustrious crowd.

Suzanne squeezed his arm lightly, and wished him well, to which he replied, "I do hope you enjoy the show. You look ravishing, darling, as always!"

Uncle Walter bowed to his audience, and then sat down at the piano with a swish of tuxedo tails. He commenced the evening with *Alexander's Ragtime Band.* As he ended the piece with a rousing flourish, the crowd responded enthusiastically, obviously enjoying his rendition of Irving Berlin's popular song. It was one of Jonathan's favorites. So many popular tunes were beloved by them both; after all, music had become inescapably intertwined with their love for each other.

April Showers, I Can't Believe That You're In Love With Me, But Not For Me, Always, and *Everybody Loves My Baby* rolled out exquisitely from the finely crafted Steinway grand piano. Suzanne grew misty eyed and dreamy, reveling in past pleasures. When Uncle Walter started playing *Blue Skies,* she was not certain she could hold back her tears though she did manage to do so.

He finished the show with *I Love a Piano* causing the crowd to erupt in raucous cheers of delight. Uncle Walter's professional debut had been a grand success. Though Uncle Walter came to say good-bye, he was soon off to celebrate with friends.

They rose late the next morning; attending church was out of the question. After breakfast, everyone lay around the house languidly resting or reading. It was going to be another hot summer day. Of course, her mother merely slowed down a bit. Grace was never languid and besides, they were having their large family Sunday dinner, as usual.

Her mother seemed rather impatient all throughout the day. Last night had been a splendid experience, enjoyed by all, Grace included. Suzanne wondered at her mother's sour mood and decided it best to stay out of the way. Still floating in a dream world, she took Rosie outside to play with Missy. Although she brought along a book to read, she continued instead with her reverie of idyllic interludes spent with Jonathan.

Early that evening, with Rosie still napping, Suzanne walked down the stairs, headed for the parlor. It was the coolest spot in the house. Completely immersed in Pearl S. Buck's newest book, *The Good Earth,* she was anxious to continue reading it.

As she neared the bottom of the staircase, Suzanne was startled to see the parlor doors closed. Voices came from within. Her father's strong voice was unmistakable, and he sounded rather stern. The other voice was muffled, making it unrecognizable. She turned to walk back upstairs, but stopped when the doors opened. Jonathan emerged with her father.

She took in the sight of him--black wavy hair, wide easy grin, compelling blue eyes, crisp shirt and sharply pressed pants--and without any forethought whatsoever, ran down the stairs and into his arms. Though obviously surprised, Jonathan immediately embraced her, tenderly whispering endearments into her softly upswept hair with its curls trailing around the nape of the neck.

"What are you . . . when did you . . . you and my father were talking?"

"I came to tell your father that I have a full time job now, to ask him if he would persuade you to . . ."

"You have a full time job?" Suzanne interrupted. "Where?"

"At the Huntington Hotel, working as a cook for Arabella's Lounge. I will be working at night, so I can still work my part time job during the day."

Pleased, but uncertain, Suzanne exclaimed, "You know how to be a restaurant cook?"

"Oh," Jonathan replied airily, "I'll learn as I go."

Her father stepped up beside Suzanne and said cautiously, "Jonathan and I have been talking about his future. He is willing to work hard and hopes you will give him another chance. I have listened to all he had to say, but told him you were the one he needed to tell these things to, though I warned him, he must take better care of Rosie and you . . . I am grateful, Jonathan, that you came to me this time."

Letting out a breath, Suzanne felt dizzy with the suddenness of Jonathan's appearance and her unexpected reaction to seeing him.

Jonathan looked down at her and asked tentatively, "Won't you come dancing with me tonight?"

Still besotted with romanticized thoughts of the past, Suzanne immediately agreed and then said, "Oh, but I am not dressed to go out dancing."

"It does not start for another hour or so. I will come back for you. You'll be the most beautiful girl in the room, I've no doubt, you always are," Jonathan said grinning deliriously.

Dressed in a black silk ankle-length, bias cut dress that fell into a smooth vertical drape that clung to her hips then flared out at the hem, Suzanne enjoyed every single moment that she danced with Jonathan. The feeling of his arms holding her across the bare back that dipped to a creamy white silk bow at her waist was delectably divine.

Too tired to talk, they simply savored being together as Jonathan made his way to her parent's house in the old roadster.

At the door, Jonathan kissed her passionately, then wisely stopped and said, "Let's go fishing with Rosie next Thursday. I won't be working that day. We can get an early start, spend the whole day together."

Seeing her hesitate, he added, "Rosie would love it and we can talk about those things you said you wanted to tell me."

Thinking of Rosie and feeling he was ready to talk seriously about their problems, Suzanne responded, "Yes, Jonathan, I would like that very much. I will see you then."

After checking on Rosie, Suzanne went directly to bed where she dreamed of dancing with Jonathan in the soft light of a tranquil moon.

October, 1931
Glendora, California

CHAPTER THIRTY-ONE

"Surely a single flute of champagne should not be affecting me so adversely this morning," Suzanne mused as she lay sleepily recounting her evening with Jonathan. "Oh, my goodness!" she exclaimed out loud, causing Rosie to stir. "It can't be."

Suzanne went into the bathroom and splashed cool water on her face as if to whisk away her thoughts. The face she saw reflected in the mirror was rather pale; her stomach rolled as another wave of nausea hit. Acknowledging to herself that her stomach had been unsettled for a couple of weeks, she counted backwards to the last night she had been with Jonathan. Although it was just over six weeks since she had left Jonathan and that dreadful house; it felt like a lifetime had passed.

Counting forward, she calculated that if she were indeed expecting, their baby would be born sometime in the Spring of next year.

Suzanne collapsed back onto the bed, very uncertain of her feelings. This most certainly complicated things, and yet . . . made the decision abundantly clear.

She thought back over the recent conversations she'd had with Jonathan. They had talked about the latest jazz songs and Jonathan's beloved Red Sox, Danny and Molly, his new job at Arabella's Lounge, Rosie's antics, the books Suzanne had been reading, but never about the incident, his altered behavior, or their own future. She had no idea just how to bring about such a conversation.

Jonathan was a master at distracting her with his charms and, it was such a painful topic. It was hard to know exactly what to do. Maybe another discussion with Grandpa Stuart would help. She would walk over to the groves later today and see if he had time to chat.

Why did life have to be so difficult to figure out anyway? If only Jonathan came from a more affluent family, if only this wretched thing they were calling "The Depression" had not happened, if only baby Johnny had not died, if only . . . well, she supposed this could go on all day. Time to buck up and figure out what she was going to do as before long, her condition would become noticeable, at least to her mother and her family. And, she could not keep the news from Jonathan very long either, it was his baby as well as hers.

"Oh," she moaned softly as she turned over, pushing her face into the monogrammed pillow.

Billowing clouds clustered in the deep blue sky as a slight breeze blew through the trees in the lemon, orange, and walnut groves bringing to Suzanne the sweet scents of the rose gardens and ripened fruit, causing her spirit to relax. What a relief that it was not as sweltering and hot as it had been for several weeks. Though Suzanne walked the length and breadth of the groves, she did not find her grandfather. Disappointed, she returned to the house.

When Cook served fish pie at dinner, Suzanne's stomach rebelled and she had to flee the table.

After Rosie was asleep, Suzanne crept to the library planning to read, only to find her father and mother sitting in there, talking.

"Ah, Suzanne, we were just discussing your future," her mother said, a strident tone marking her voice. "We were wondering what could have possibly made you bolt from the table so unceremoniously tonight, though it is not hard to guess at the truth."

Suzanne groaned inwardly and wished she had stayed in her own suite. Her patience worn thin from the incessant thoughts she'd been pondering all day along with the constant nausea, Suzanne snapped, "Mother, I have told you that I am not ready to make a decision yet. Jonathan has a full time job now and is ready to support us. Besides, you have probably guessed, I think that I might be pregnant again."

Her mother was shocked at her use of such a vulgar term in front of her father, "Suzanne, watch your language, you are a lady."

It seemed such an insignificant detail to Suzanne. What was

the use in calling a simple reality by a more "genteel" name--the fact of the matter was that she was most likely pregnant.

"Well, this is a fine kettle of fish you have gotten yourself into," her mother continued testily.

The giggles started in her belly and erupted from her throat before she could stop them. Her father caught the irony and winked at her.

"Just what is so humorous about that statement?" her mother queried.

"Grace, it was the smell of the fish pie at dinner that made Suzanne ill. Don't you see the humor in the fact that you used the term 'kettle of fish'?"

"This is not a situation to laugh about; adding another child to Suzanne's burdens is not humorous. Marriage is hard enough without adding baby after baby to the situation," her mother stated sourly.

"Mother, I do not consider Rosie a burden! Jonathan loves having babies and so do I," Suzanne exclaimed defiantly.

"Obviously," her mother shot back, "he keeps right on producing them in spite of the fact that he cannot properly care for them."

"Rosie has always been well cared for. Maybe she has not lived in luxury, but she has never gone without anything she needed. And, she is ever so loved by both of us."

"Well, we love Rosie, too, and we want what is best for her."

"What is best for her is being with both of her parents and that means Jonathan," Suzanne practically shouted.

All the bridges built over the past few weeks between mother and daughter disintegrated as iron wills clashed fiercely, one against the other.

"Suzanne, you have no way to support yourself or your own child. Jonathan is ill-equipped to do so."

"Well, maybe if you had allowed me to go to college like I wanted to do, my life would be different. I felt trapped . . . like I had no other choice, but to marry as you so firmly told me I must do. So I did and I wanted to marry Jonathan. I love him . . . he makes me happy! Jonathan is Rosie's father, he's my husband, he'll be the father of my new baby, and I am leaving to live with him again, as soon as possible." Suzanne responded angrily as she felt herself losing complete control.

Her mother was about to continue when her father stepped in, "Grace, we do not want Suzanne to lose the baby because of this unbearable tension. Everyone needs to calm down before that happens."

His words brought them both quickly to their senses. Suzanne could not imagine going through another such loss. Grace gasped and stated,   "Of course not, I have said too much."

"Suzanne, it is not necessary for you to make a hasty decision," her father said soothingly. "You may stay here as long as you wish, even if you are expecting another child. Grace, this is not the time to push her into a decision. It will simply result in continuing complication for us all. Let her be."

Knowing her father would pay a price for standing up to her mother, Suzanne went to stand beside him. She laid a delicate hand on his strong arm and spoke calmly, "I have been thinking all day about things and I still feel rather confused. Jonathan has a job now and that makes things different. Of course, the possibility of a new baby also changes the situation. However, I have not had a chance to talk with him as I wish to do, about his drinking, his terrible moodiness and all of that. Please, I need some more time."

Feeling rather faint, Suzanne perched at the edge of an oversized chair as she continued, "Thank you, father, for saying I can stay. I have been happy being here with the family again. You have been very good to me these past few weeks . . . Mother, your help with Rosie has been most appreciated. Father . . . you've provided so many nice extras for Rosie and me which has been so very wonderful. I do love you both. Yet, I must face up to reality. I am trying to make the right decision for everyone concerned."

Exhausted and feeling nauseous once again, Suzanne stood and before her mother could say another word, she hastily left the room and dashed up the stairs to her bedroom.

Feeling wounded and ever so weary, she prepared for bed, hoping a good night sleep would bring a clearer mind tomorrow. Dropping off to sleep, she felt some of the words that she had heard at baby Johnny's funeral flutter through her mind, "Come unto me all you who are weary and find rest for your soul."

October, 1931
Glendora, California

CHAPTER THIRTY-TWO

Autumn had hopscotched across the region. In Southern California, the fall foliage does not arrive full blown; it has to be sought out to be enjoyed.

Suzanne and Rosie spent several fun-filled days with Jonathan, driving about the multi-hued countryside, looking for leaves burnished gold, pumpkin, and scarlet, often stopping along the way for a picnic. To Rosie's absolute delight, one Saturday Jonathan came very early and they all went fishing together. On other days, they simply went for long walks among the foothills of the San Gabriel Mountains. When Rosie grew tired, Jonathan would carry her. They sang, they laughed, and they lay again among the wild lavender and sage, taking delight in each other as Rosie napped.

Jonathan took her dancing again, twice. Never once did he drink to excess or treat her roughly. Instead, he spoke tenderly of his love for her, complimenting her clothes and her loveliness. As always, they danced every dance together, jubilantly reveling in each moment. This was the Jonathan that she loved – effervescent, boisterous, charming, full of merriment, and solicitous.

Danny and Molly moved into their own apartment where they anxiously awaited the birth of their firstborn. Although it was not socially acceptable for Molly to go out in public, Jonathan and Suzanne went to visit them. Oh, how the two couples delighted in being together again. One night, they draped Molly's growing tummy as artfully as possible and crept ever so casually into the movie theater. No one took notice of Molly's bulging form and thus they avoided scandalizing the sensibilities of the public. They laughed all the way home over the antics of the Marx Brothers in *Monkey Business*.

Although Suzanne made it abundantly clear she would not return to live with Jonathan's mother, she never again brought up Jonathan's dreadful behavior or baby Johnny. It was too hard a task to break into their rhapsodic moments with such painful reminders of their former troubles. While in each other company, Suzanne and Jonathan simply floated along with the currents of joyful abandonment. All was well. Jonathan had returned to his former self. It was all that was needed; surely it was best to avoid the tedium of reliving the past.

Dr. Stevens had confirmed her suspicions and Suzanne knew she must soon tell Jonathan of the coming event. She was not sure just how he would react, but was fairly certain that, as always, he would be ecstatic.

Telling him, however, meant a decision had to be made; after all, this was his baby too. In spite of the grand times they'd had together the past several weeks, Suzanne was still unable to make up her mind about the future.

Grandpa Stuart was heavily involved in a harvest cycle, and Suzanne realized he would not be available to talk for a long while. Her tenderhearted father could not be relied upon for advice; he would simply say he wanted her to be happy. There was no doubt, at all, about her mother's position on the matter. Suzanne knew she would be showing soon and as such, the decision would then be thrust upon her.

No matter, she would think this through on her own. She was 21 years old and a mother, capable of making up her own mind.

Needing to be alone to mull things over, Suzanne arranged to use Edward's Model A sports coupe for the day. She left Rosie with Grandmother Stuart and took off for a drive in the countryside. It was a rare treat for Suzanne to drive, let alone go anywhere alone. Though a little nervous, she felt ready for an adventure and a challenge. She took along a picnic lunch, a blanket, a book, and plenty of water.

Taking Route 66, she drove west, and then veered north until she reached the foothills. Not particularly certain of where she was going, Suzanne decided to travel west again, she knew Pasadena was in that direction. Driving along the foothills, she spotted a large park filled with lush foliage, huge trees and many people--families, couples, dogs, and loners like herself. She parked the coupe and headed for a shady spot that afforded her some privacy.

After spreading out her blanket, she leaned up against a tree and read. After a while she ate her lunch, dozed off for a bit, woke with a start and thought about reading some more, but then stopped herself.

"It is time to think. That is what I came here to do."

Her mind felt like a blank slate. Nothing came. With a sigh, she packed everything back into the Model A and wondered what to do next.

"It is a lovely day, not too hot, the park is lush and extensive, there are plenty of people about, why don't I walk for a bit," she decided.

The beauty of her surroundings, the warmth of the sun, and the fresh air refreshed Suzanne, bringing clarity to her spirit. As though playing out on a movie screen, various days and delights from their time at the little cottage flashed into her mind. In a burst of recognition, she began to understand.

"It is the adventure of life that I want. My parent's home is secure and while there, I have need of nothing. Yet, I languish; I feel barely alive, even with Rosie occasionally kicking things up."

She kept walking and pondered further, "I love being with my family, but I dislike the social sphere my parents relish. The predictability is monotonous; it leaves no room for anything out of the ordinary or anyone that is different. I want to be stimulated.

Life with Jonathan is rarely predictable, yet I love it that way. He makes me laugh, he makes me think, he makes me feel alive."

The faster her mind assimilated these new thoughts, the faster she walked. The faster she walked, the clearer things became. It was time. It was time to return to the life she had chosen when she married Jonathan, regardless of the difficulties.

"As long as we stay away from Maggie Mae and that house, I believe we will make it. We can visit my family. I will go to see them regularly and Jonathan will just have to understand that is what I want to do. But, we can live our own lives, carve out our own way."

She understood now that she would never be truly happy living out her life in the shadows; well cared for, yet never reaching inside of herself to meet life head on, straining with effort, growing stronger and wiser in the process.

"One thing is certain--life with Jonathan will not be easy. Nevertheless, it is the right decision for me. I need to see Jonathan right away and tell him he is going to be a father again. I need to give him time to find a home for us. I need to explain how I feel about my family and being with them more often. I need to make him realize that though I may be returning to live with him again, he must never ever mistreat me again--maybe being apart for so long has helped him really understand that. Most of all, we need time together, the three of us, readjusting to each other before this baby is born."

She felt settled now and ready to proceed with life. It was time to go back and tell her parents. Suzanne headed for the sports coupe to drive back to Glendora, to her parent's home, and to the gardens and groves that she loved. Most importantly, she was headed home--home to Jonathan.

CHAPTER THIRTY-THREE

"Jonathan," Suzanne spoke quietly, "I have something to tell you. Let's go take a walk in the gardens."

Charles had insisted that Grace invite Jonathan for their Sunday afternoon family dinner. Mother had grudgingly acquiesced, though her displeasure at Jonathan was evident in the set of her jaw and the scowl on her face whenever she glanced at him. Fortunately, Jonathan was so busy talking with her cousins, aunts, and uncles that he did not appear to notice.

"I go walk too," Rosie said, hopping up and down vigorously as they headed for the front door. Suzanne knew it would be more difficult to talk with Rosie along, yet realized that to leave her behind would create a scene, drawing attention to their exit, which is exactly what she was trying to avoid.

"Okay, Rosie girl, you can come, but mama wants to talk to daddy. Will you be a good girl and play with Missy out in the garden?"

"I play ball wif Missy," Rosie said happily as she toddled along beside Jonathan.

As they strolled along the brick path skirting the groves,

Jonathan held Rosie by one hand as he circled Suzanne's waist with the other. He looked rather apprehensive about the proposed talk, so Suzanne said, "Let's head back to the gardens."

Rosie made it clear she wanted to keep walking, but Suzanne promised to tell her a secret if she played nicely with Missy for a little while. Rosie loved secrets, so readily settled into a game of fetch with Missy.

As they sat down together on the ornate wrought iron settee, Jonathan kissed Suzanne lightly on the cheek as he caressed her hand, speaking gently, "Honey, you and Rosie are my darlin' girls, you will always be the loves of my life!"

"Oh, how you do like to charm me, dearest Jonathan."

He seemed to relax a bit as he asked, "What did you want to talk to me about, Suzanne?"

"I read once that Mark Twain said to '. . . throw off the boundaries, sail away from the safe harbor. Catch the trade winds . . . Explore, Dream, Discover . . .' it is what I am meant to do."

Jonathan looked puzzled and somewhat fearful at her words.

"I have come to realize it is time for me to stop hiding away in the sure harbor of my parent's home. I'm ready to explore life with you again, live out the adventure . . . discover the paths we are meant to walk together." Then she added softly with a little smile, "Find our skies of blue."

To Suzanne's great surprise, it looked like Jonathan was about to cry. Barely able to speak he told her, "I have missed you so much! Life has been horribly dull and without meaning since you went away."

"There is one more thing . . . I . . . um, Rosie come here to mama, I have something to tell you . . . we, uh . . . Rosie come right now, mama wants to tell you . . . I'm going to tell you the secret now."

Rosie dropped the ball and ran to her parents. Jonathan scooped her into his arms and placed her on his knee.

"We are going to have another baby, Jonathan . . . Rosie, would you like to have a baby brother or a baby sister come to live with us?"

For once, Jonathan was speechless; though, once he assimilated the news, he stood up, grabbed Suzanne and waltzed around the garden with Rosie between them.

"We'll have a little boy. We'll have lots of fun together-- goin' fishing, goin' camping, hiking, playing ball . . . I'll teach him how to play baseball, to love the Red Sox, and build things, and oh, there are so many things that we'll do together . . ."

Rosie appeared not quite certain what her parents were so excited about, though she gleefully clapped her hands anyway.

Suzanne leaned against Jonathan and sighed, "I am so relieved that you are happy about this."

"Why would you think anything else? It's the best news ever, Suzanne! Rosie girl, you are going to have a brother or maybe a sister, but I think a brother. Isn't that the greatest thing you ever heard about?" Jonathan practically shouted.

"Jonathan, we have to think about where we are going to live, you know we can't live with your mother again, we cannot. I will not go back to live in that house ever again!"

"I know, you told me. I understand. I've been trying to save money. I don't have enough yet, though," Jonathan said defensively.

"It's okay . . . you just need to keep working on it. I will tell my parents about our talk today and tell them Rosie and I have to stay here a little bit longer. I will let them know that you are working on it. But, you are going to need to conserve and save money for us, Jonathan. And, maybe . . . yes, I think that you should give me the money you have saved up or give it to my father or to Grandfather Hughes. Actually, I am sure that is what we should do about the money. You know, Jonathan that you have rather a hard time saving money."

At first, Jonathan looked like he was going to get angry at what she proposed. However, his attitude changed very quickly as he looked at Rosie and then at Suzanne.

"You are right. I will bring it over for you to hang onto . . . It's not much yet, Suzanne. I need to be with my girls. I know that I need to do whatever it takes to make that happen fast," Jonathan said most humbly, and then added, "Let's go celebrate, let's get an ice cream soda at the drugstore or something."

Hand in hand, they walked to the old roadster as Rosie nestled sleepily in Suzanne's arms, worn out from the long day and all the excitement.

As they walked into the drugstore together, the radio was playing *Always*. Suzanne smiled up at Jonathan and he grinned back at her, making her heart flutter with anticipation.

CHAPTER THIRTY-FOUR

On March 23, 1932, Suzanne delivered a healthy baby boy who ate voraciously and cried lustily. She was overjoyed to see their baby so obviously healthy and strong. Once again, Jonathan carried the baby all over the hospital to show off his son with immense pride. Suzanne let Jonathan pick his name, and Jonathan named the baby--Robert Charles Kelly.

"We'll call him Bobby," Jonathan said tenderly to Suzanne as she lay resting. "He can be Robert Charles when he's a man, but for now, he's our little Bobby. Thank you, honey, for having us a son."

When her parents came to visit, Grace was thrilled over the baby's middle name.

"It was certainly considerate of you to honor your father, especially under the circumstances."

"I am glad you are happy about it, Mother. Jonathan chose the name for the baby."

"I see," Grace said rather icily, then stopped herself and smiled slightly. "I suppose Jonathan is grateful."

"He is."

After her parents left, Danny stopped by to visit for a few minutes, then left with Jonathan. As the baby lay sleeping, Suzanne knew she should sleep too, yet could not stop mulling over the events of the past several months.

Just after she had informed Jonathan they were about to have another baby, Grandpa Stuart suggested to her parents that they let Jonathan come to live with them until after the baby was born. Grandpa said Jonathan would benefit from exposure to Suzanne's family and the lifestyle to which she was accustomed. Suzanne's father agreed, adding that it made much more sense for Suzanne's well being also.

Though her mother had changed for the better, Suzanne was incredulous when she agreed to such an arrangement. Suzanne was almost certain it was because of Rosie, nevertheless was relieved to have their housing matter resolved for the time being.

As an impetus toward securing a home for his family, Grandpa Stuart and Suzanne's father informed Jonathan that they would match dollar for dollar all that he was able to save toward the goal.

Grandfather Hughes refused to be involved as he was of the opinion that Jonathan should learn the banking business so he could come to work at the bank. Everyone else realized the absurdity of such an expectation; Jonathan was not cut out to be a business man and especially not a banker. However, Suzanne was told in confidence, that Grandmother Hughes was "working on talking some sense" into her husband.

For the most part, things had gone smoothly over the course of the past five months. It helped a lot that Jonathan was working so many hours and rarely underfoot while her mother was about the house. However, there were moments when her mother's resolve to change disintegrated into extreme irritation over Jonathan's lack of refinement.

"Is he not capable of understanding?" she would ask at such times.

"Grace, he is trying. Do you not see that? He cannot be expected to change overnight," her father would intervene. "It seems to me a certain lady has determined to treat others more kindly, yet falters at times," he would say without rancor.

"Yes, Charles, you are absolutely right," her mother would respond as she set her jaw with determination. "I must try harder to get along with Jonathan."

"What an amazing sight to behold," Suzanne would muse. "Something certainly has taken hold of my mother."

In early December of last year, the entire family had gathered to celebrate Rosie's second birthday. Miss Rose Ann Kelly thrived in the spotlight and thus kept everyone laughing at her charming antics the whole day through. Christmas Day had been most pleasant. Almost as lavish as usual, though Grace made an effort to tone things down a bit in recognition of the ongoing economic depression. To Suzanne's great surprise, Grandma Stuart told her that the money saved had been donated by Grace to charities that were helping those who were struggling or out of work.

Molly had delivered her baby late in January, a little boy who was named after his father. Little Dan, as they called him, was an easy going baby. Molly and Danny were ecstatic about parenthood. Molly was so enchanted with the baby that she rarely left his side. Suzanne went to visit a couple of times, feeling fortunate each time that she managed to avoid contact with Maggie Mae.

As Suzanne's thoughts came back into the present, she snuggled baby Bobby close and breathed a sigh of relief over his robustness. Surely it was a sign of good things to come . . . surely happiness and prosperity were just around the corner for her little family.

Rosie was overjoyed when Suzanne and Jonathan brought her "bruver" home to stay. However, once she realized how much attention baby Bobby was getting, she found ways to grab everyone's attention, some of which were delightful while others were outright naughty. Suzanne was ever so grateful for the help of her mother, grandmothers, and the household staff in caring for the children.

When Bobby was just two months old, Grandfather Hughes announced during the Sunday afternoon family dinner that the bank had been forced to foreclose on a house near Willow Springs Park. He excitedly told everyone that the house would be perfect for Suzanne and Jonathan's little family. Within just a few weeks, financing had been secured for the balance due on the mortgage and cast-off furniture had been obtained from various friends and family members.

Grandpa Stuart lent his trucks and workers for the move, Grace helped out with unpacking and arranging furniture, and Grandma Stuart came to make curtains and bring canned goods and other staples from her pantry. Grandmother Hughes would not sully her hands with such work, but lent her maid for several days of cleaning.

"What a difference from the time we moved by ourselves to the cottage," Suzanne thought as she watched her family working together. Suzanne was still regaining her strength and as such, ever so grateful the help. "Jonathan has won their hearts as he did mine. Well, at least my mother tolerates him now."

Jonathan, Suzanne, Rosie, and baby Bobby settled into the small, albeit comfortable home. Suzanne set out to make it feel as cozy as the cottage. Jonathan immediately planted a garden in the hopes of procuring a late summer harvest.

Rosie undeniably missed the various people and workers always flowing through her grandparents' home; she especially missed her grandparents and Missy, the dog. However, she rapidly adjusted. Fascinated as baby Bobby grew bigger, Rosie was soon absorbed with life on Fountain Springs Lane.

It was June, nearly her 22nd birthday. Suzanne sat drinking some of Grandpa Stuart's lemonade as she watched Rosie playing in the backyard while baby Bobby slept alongside her. Relaxed and happy, she thought of what F. Scott Fitzgerald had written in his book, *The Great Gatsby* ~

   "I had that familiar conviction that life was beginning over again with the summer."

July, 1932
Glendora, California

CHAPTER THIRTY-FIVE

Reality fell on Suzanne like a star falling from the heavens; shining brightly, yet overwhelmingly heavy. She had quickly forgotten just how much work was involved in maintaining a home. There were all those months at her parents with servants and hired hands taking care of everything. Before that, at Maggie Mae's the housework and cooking had been shared.

Now, she was struggling just to keep up with the basics-- cooking, cleaning, and child care. The summer heat made it all that much harder to accomplish anything.

Jonathan was gone to work so very much of the time. When he was at home, he was understandably tired. Day after day Suzanne struggled along with the enormous workload. Sometimes, she felt as though life was crushing her into a one-dimensional version of herself. Rosie was often bored and in an effort to gain Suzanne's attention, she would misbehave.

"Maybe we should get a dog to help keep Rosie entertained," she thought one afternoon, then groaned at the thought of the extra work that would involve. "She needs someone to play with, a little friend."

Suzanne hesitated to talk with Jonathan about it all; he was obviously trying so hard to live up to her expectations. At times, her family was helping them out, yet they needed to tend their own homes and each had busy lives to lead. She missed her old neighbors, Harvey and Mary and the wonderful times they had spent together. The thought gave her an idea. She should find a way to get to know the people in this neighborhood.

"Jonathan, we need to get to know our neighbors. Let's invite everyone on the street over for a backyard picnic. We could ask them all to bring something to share, you could fry some chicken. Maybe Grandpa Stuart could bring over some lemonade and Grandma Stuart some of her pies. What do you say? I get awfully lonely sometimes when you are gone so much . . . and, it would be helpful to know our neighbors . . . don't you think?"

"Sure. Sounds good to me. Let's plan it soon. How about a Saturday afternoon early next month? If I ask in advance, I can trade off with someone and get the day off work."

A date was set. Rosie skipped alongside Suzanne as she walked with baby Bobby in her arms to deliver invitations to each door on their street. Several families accepted the invitation and so preparations commenced. The heat and humidity was exhausting. However, Suzanne was so excited about the picnic that she found a way. Jonathan was excited, too, as he put the backyard in tip top shape.

The picnic was a huge success. Everyone seemed grateful

for the opportunity to socialize. Danny and Molly came with little Dan as well as four families from the neighborhood.

Jonathan and Suzanne found their next door neighbors, Max and Martha, were a vivacious couple with grown children. In spite of their age difference, the two couples had a lot in common-- they loved to dance, they liked playing cards, and they were big baseball fans. Another family that came from down the street had a little boy named Roger who was just a few months older than Rosie. All during the afternoon their two little heads--one blonde and one brown--could be seen side by side, playing contentedly. One couple was retired and traveled a lot. However, they seemed very pleasant to know. The last couple was a pair of newlyweds who had eyes only for each other.

As summer headed towards its end, the unbearable heat dissipated and Suzanne grew more accustomed to the work of tending a home and children by herself. Nevertheless, she always felt so tired and longed for respite. On rare days when her mother was not busy, she would send Ramon to pick up Suzanne, Rosie, and baby Bobby. He would whisk them away to her parent's house. Her mother or Grandma Stuart would watch the children so Suzanne could enjoy a heavenly afternoon sitting and reading in the garden.

Suzanne soon cultivated a friendship with Roger's mother, Ann, who had a car available to drive during the day. The two women would sometimes set off for the park or downtown for an afternoon of adventure. Rosie and Roger could play together happily for hours.

One evening, just as Jonathan was arriving home for dinner, Max came over to invite them to a square dance at a local barn in Pasadena. Suzanne immediately told him she did not think it possible. However, Jonathan intervened, "You could use a break from the children and housework, Suzanne. Let's see if Molly or your mom or Ann will watch the children. Let's go, it would be good for us."

"Well, Max, I guess if we can find someone to watch the children, we'll join you. We've done a lot of dancing, but square dancing will be a new one for us. Can you come over before Saturday and show us some of the steps?"

"Sure, we'd love to. Just name the time."

Jonathan and Suzanne immediately took to the rhythms of square dancing; each found the experience enjoyable and exhilarating.

Occasionally, Max and Martha would suggest a game of cards. Martha would call to say that they were headed over to play a few hands. Suzanne would fuss over the state of the house and think of reasons why they shouldn't; while Jonathan, always ready for fun, would swing her around and around, telling her to leave the dishes and the housework so she could celebrate life with their friends.

Suzanne would start giggling and then realize he was right. Both Suzanne and Jonathan found such refreshment in those evenings filled with hilarity.

The Red Sox had another poor season. However, Jonathan followed the World Series with gusto and was delighted that the Yankees swept the Cubs in four games. His hero, Babe Ruth, outshone Lou Gehrig despite their matched talent for hitting home runs. In game three, Ruth and Gehrig each hit a home run in the fifth inning (in back-to-back at-bats), but it was Ruth's hit that garnered national attention when he "predicted" his home run. During the at-bat, Ruth made a pointing gesture to the center field bleachers. On the next pitch, he hit a home run deep to center field, past the flagpole and into the temporary seating, for an estimated distance of nearly 500 feet. However, conflicting testimony and inconclusive film footage kept newspaper men and baseball fans arguing about the validity of his prediction for weeks.

In November, Franklin Delano Roosevelt was elected as President. During his campaign he had promised he would battle the economic depression with a platform proclaiming he would pursue relief, recovery and reform. People all over the nation were encouraged by his vow:

"I pledge myself to a new deal for the American people."

Jonathan and Suzanne hoped that meant economic relief would follow for their family. Though they were making it, Jonathan worked long, long hours each week. Additionally, many rumors were flying about the future of Arabella's Lounge at the Huntington Hotel.

Though the sun was out, the wind made it a chilly afternoon on the very last day of November. Suzanne sat watching

Rosie and Roger play in the yard. Surprised, she looked up to find Jonathan standing beside her, his face ashen and constricted.

"Jonathan, you're home! Whatever is the matter?"

"It's little Dan. Molly couldn't wake him up from his nap. He's dead, he's dead, Suzanne, just like baby Johnny, he's dead."

Suzanne could not move. It was the nightmare happening all over again.

"My Ma was over visiting Molly. Danny was at work. Little Dan was taking his morning nap. Ma told Molly to take a break, go for a walk, said Molly needed to let his grandmamma take care of him sometimes . . . so, Molly went for a short walk. When she came home, she thought it strange that little Dan wasn't up from his nap yet, so she went to check on him. That's when she found him. After the sheriff came and they took baby Dan away, Danny came to get me at work. He's all shook up, but Molly is inconsolable."

"I have to go see her, now."

"I knew you'd want to go. I called your father at the bank, told him what happened, said we needed help with the kids. He's headed over here with your mother. Let's get Roger home so when they get here, we can go see Danny and Molly," Jonathan told her, then put his head down and moaned ever so softly, "I should've known, I should've seen it coming."

"Jonathan, everyone, even the doctors and nurses told us these things happen, there is no way to predict them. The babies aren't healthy enough or something, they just stop breathing. How could you have known it would happen to little Dan? It's just a coincidence that it happened to Molly and Danny's baby too. There's no way you could have seen it coming."

"You don't understand, but that's okay, I don't really understand either," Jonathan raised his head, and then continued hopefully. "Maybe you're right. Maybe, it is just a coincidence. I have to believe that." Yet, his eyes looked extremely troubled.

Suzanne's heart constricted; it was the same look he'd had after baby Johnny died. It was a look beyond grief; it was a look of utter torment. It made her feel so very afraid.

Even reminding her that baby Danny was up in heaven with baby Johnny did little to assuage Molly's torrent of grief. Jonathan was right--she was inconsolable. Suzanne felt so very helpless, and it felt like the torn places in her heart started to bleed again. She thought again about the words said by the preacher on the day of baby Johnny's funeral. Then she wondered once more whether they were true, wondered if she was ever going to find peace that lasted.

And, Jonathan went out drinking that night; he did not come home until dawn.

CHAPTER THIRTY-SIX

Life seemed to be crumbling around Suzanne like the dry dirt clods she liked to pick up and hurl when she was a kid, running through the groves with her cousins.

Molly, the one who had given her hope when baby Johnny died, was completely at a standstill. She could not seem to recover from the death of little Dan. On the other hand, Danny had taken to going out drinking every night with Jonathan. The two would stagger home in the early morning hours, either singing lustily at the top of their lungs or cursing the world in general.

Danny and Molly decided against having a funeral for little Dan, both saying they could not bear the thought of watching their baby lowered into the ground. As such, little Dan was interred in private, his gravesite a spot right next to little Johnny's.

The Sheriff's office closed its investigation; the matter ruled as an unexplained, but natural death. Suzanne hoped the decision would bring some rest to Molly's soul.

Christmas grew closer and Suzanne realized they had not seen Molly for several weeks. As such, she decided it was time to pay her a visit.

Leaving Rosie and baby Bobby with her new friend Ann, Suzanne took the bus over to see Molly. Upon entering the house, she was shocked at what she saw. There were things strewn in disarray everywhere throughout the house while Molly looked disheveled, ashen, and haggard.

"I'm goin' back home to Ireland," Molly said as she scooped clothing off the sofa so Suzanne could sit down. "Danny and his family are cursed . . . I'm sure of it. Two babies dying, one right after another--it has to be a curse. It is the curse of the Banshee. I am certain I heard her keenin' the night before little Dan died, I should have known, should have taken him then and there, away . . . far away from this horrible place. Oh! Why did I not listen? Oh, why didn't I do something?"

Suzanne sat in stunned silence, and then finally ventured a question. "Who is the Banshee?"

"She's an Irish spirit from the "otherworld," a frightful fairy woman dressed in white sheeting with long, flowing silvery hair . . . she comes from the woodlands to warn of death, she attaches herself to certain clans . . . families that she picks out to haunt. It is Maggie Mae, she brought the curse of the Banshee with her from Ireland, I'm sure of it."

Trying to assimilate the information she was hearing, Suzanne thought of what she had read about fairies--delightful little creatures with soft musical voices that giggled and flew about on shimmering wings. She remembered something that J.M. Barrie wrote in his book called *Peter Pan:*

"When the first baby laughed for the first time, its laugh broke into a thousand pieces, and they all went skipping about, and that was the beginning of fairies."

Suzanne could not quite picture such adorable creatures looking like the woman that Molly was describing. But, of this she was certain, Molly absolutely believed Danny's family was cursed; that this was in fact the reason for little Dan's death. Thinking quickly, Suzanne used every means she could to dissuade Molly. Nevertheless, her efforts were to no avail.

Exhausted from the hard work, Suzanne returned home where she sat down and cried, wondering, "What will become of Danny?"

Two days later, Jonathan found a note from Danny, slipped under the front door stating that he could not bear life without Molly. It said he wanted to be anywhere else, said he was heading out to see Uncle Gerard in Arizona. Jonathan doubled over and gripped his stomach in pain as he cried out, "Where will it all end?" When he looked up at Suzanne, his eyes were hard and filled with rage. He quickly looked away, leaving Suzanne feeling chilled and scared.

For Rosie's sake, Suzanne wanted the holidays to be festive. It was, after all, their first Christmas in their very own house. She put on the radio where Christmas songs played merrily. She found a small tree that she let Rosie trim with colorful balls and then they added bright lights. Suzanne wrapped presents in colorful paper to put under the tree, much to Rosie's curious delight.

Rosie was now three years old and she liked helping out with the baking. She patted the flour, rolled the dough and decorated the cookies, in a clumsy sort of way, while chattering and singing the entire time. Suzanne found Rosie's good cheer a solace to her aching heart. Fortunately, baby Bobby was cooperative during these activities--taking his nap on cue, playing happily in his crib for a bit after he woke and generally bringing sunshine to their home.

Although her parents, aunts and uncles, cousins and grandparents were saddened about Danny and Molly's loss of family, they had not been particularly close to them and so carried on as usual with their holiday festivities. Suzanne felt comforted in the swirl of family activities and enjoyed the high-spirited hilarity of her cousins. Jonathan, however, remained distant. He acted out the part of a doting father and loving husband, yet Suzanne felt the difference. His eyes were cold and his actions measured, she sensed his detachment and she became saddened by it.

Christmas Day was over and after they put the children to bed, Jonathan disappeared into the night. Suzanne, dispirited and lonely, drank some homemade wine and listened to Louis Armstrong's big band play love songs on the radio. She looked out at the moonlit sky and wondered, "Jonathan, how can I break through that hard wall you've built around your heart? Whatever will I do . . . and, how will I live without the comfort of your love?"

The next morning, Jonathan stumbled in around 10:00 a.m. looking rumpled, morose, and bleary-eyed. He hollered out for Suzanne to get him some breakfast and swore at the sun for being too bright. He yelled an obscenity when baby Bobby cried, and crashed into the kitchen wall as he lurched toward a chair. When Rosie saw this, she ran and hid behind Suzanne, crying out lustily in fear.

Looking startled, Jonathan let out a curse and sprinted awkwardly from the house. In desperation, Suzanne telephoned Grandpa Stuart, hoping he would have some sage advice, though Suzanne felt little hope that there was anything that would have a lasting effect on Jonathan.

It seemed the day dragged on and on as Suzanne attempted to soothe Rosie, feed baby Bobby and keep up a good front while tending to the housework. Extremely dispirited and anxiously pondering the future, Suzanne felt as cantankerous as her mother could be and as old as both her grandmothers were--put together!

Hours later, Jonathan came home, supported by Grandpa Stuart, looking extremely scared and rather forlorn.

"Suzie girl," Jonathan said dropping to his knees, "I've messed things up again," he told her with a slight sob in his voice. "Your grandfather's been talking to me. I told him . . . told him about how Rosie cried when she saw me. Suzie, that tore up my heart, made me hate how I've acted lately . . . made me hate myself . . . what kind of father makes his little girl cry and run away in fear when she sees him? I wanna try again, I do, I wanna try again,

Suzie girl."

Suzanne recoiled and turned away, not certain at all how she felt about Jonathan any more. She wanted to run, run far away to some place, any place, where breezes blew gently and life was serene. She felt an anger growing inside her that she was not certain she could control. She had worked so hard at all this and yet, things kept happening to undermine their efforts. Once again, it felt like they were just a little family of bluebirds twirling in a giant whirlwind.

She turned to answer Jonathan, but before she could get a word out, Grandfather said sharply, "Jonathan, I think you'd better go sleep this off. Think about what I said. Think before you act!"

As Jonathan staggered into the bedroom, Suzanne searched her grandfather's face.

"What did you say, Grandpa, what did you say to him?"

"I think that's best left between Jonathan and me, dear heart. I think he got the point. Let him get some sleep, let me know if things don't improve . . . please, do let me know, right away!"

Trying her best to feel hopeful, Suzanne watched her grandfather drive away. She was tempted to put on the radio, drink some more wine and dream of the past so she could forget the horrible hours that had just passed.

However, Suzanne's sense of duty to her children rose up; she worked to put aside her worries and her apprehensions as she carried on with her heart heavy and full of dread.

CHAPTER THIRTY-SEVEN

All throughout January and February, rain poured out of the skies bringing gloom to the little house on Fountain Springs Lane. Jonathan was working long hours to keep the family finances afloat. Baby Bobby needed constant watching as he was now crawling and getting into everything.

The rain made it difficult to keep things clean and tidy, as the children could not go outside to play; causing the pent up energy Rosie had to become unnerving. Family and friends seemed to be staying home, out of the stormy weather. Suzanne missed them, but she especially missed Molly causing her to feel isolated, lonely, and depressed.

Late in February, Suzanne had a battle with bronchitis that everyone feared would turn into pneumonia. Doctor Stevens put her to bed for a week. Fortunately, her family took turns coming over to help with the children and the housework. Jonathan took one day off work to help out, and by the end of the week, she had recuperated--tired, but having avoided another bout of pneumonia.

March came, bringing windy gales that cleared the skies, but not Suzanne's depression. March was, after all, the month in which baby Johnny had died. Additionally, she felt ever so tired; it was hard to understand why. Bobby was now sleeping through the night, and as his first birthday approached, was settling into being a placid, quiet child. Multiple rainy days had forced Rosie to learn to play quietly by herself. She would spend long hours tending her varied rag dolls--mothering them, feeding them, singing to them, and "teaching" them their ABC's. Sometimes, she allowed her friend Roger to join in the fun, but only if he listened carefully to Rosie's instructions.

On March 4, 1933, Franklin D. Roosevelt had taken the oath of President. The American people hoped and waited for him to implement the "New Deal" he had promised the economically devastated nation.

Though Jonathan was often away from home working late, he had curtailed his nights out drinking. He generally came home well before midnight without having imbibed an inordinate amount of alcohol. Nevertheless, the intensity and tenderness of their love had not returned. Suzanne found it hard to trust him and she was not sure if she really even loved him anymore. Jonathan appeared locked in another world, a world where Suzanne was not welcome. The only time she felt connected to their youthful, passionate selves was when they would go out dancing.

Fortunately, and in spite of her own frigidity toward Jonathan, Grace seemed to understand the absolute necessity for

Suzanne and Jonathan to get out for an evening together. As such, when asked, she was willing to babysit. Every few Saturday nights, Jonathan and Suzanne would drop the children off at her parent's home where they would stay until the family gathered for Sunday afternoon dinner. Grace was excited for the opportunity to take Rosie to church. Grandmother Stuart would usually care for little Bobby, thrilled at the chance to spend time with him.

They danced the Jitterbug and the Shag, they learned the Lambeth Walk and the Rumba, and sometimes they went square dancing with their neighbors, Max and Martha. Occasionally, they would see a movie or have a leisurely dinner and game of cards with Max and Martha.

However, once the evening was over, Jonathan retreated, leaving Suzanne feeling adrift and alone. The fleeting merriment left her longing for their former intimacy--times of talking late into the night about the kids' antics or their future or walking mountain paths to find a meadow where they could lay among the wildflowers, dreaming together. Thoughts of those times would kindle a glimmer of hope in Suzanne's heart that they could find their way back to loving each other again instead of just existing together in the same house.

After one especially enjoyable Saturday evening together, Suzanne asked, "Oh, Jonathan, let's go for a walk in the mountains tomorrow morning. We would have time before we go to my parent's for Sunday dinner. We could get up early . . . maybe see the sunrise, have our breakfast picnic style . . . go find a meadow and . . ."

"No," Jonathan said crossly. "I am tired from working, need to sleep in late. It is easier when the kids aren't here for me to get some extra rest. Don't you realize how hard I am working, Suzanne?"

"Don't you realize how hard I am working, Jonathan, trying to keep things clean and orderly? Do you not realize how lonely it gets being here day after day with just the kids, trying to keep them entertained? Don't you understand how much it takes out of me to economize, conserve our funds?"

"Well, you are still at home, doing what you want, when you want . . . you don't have to be at someone's beck and call, always telling you what to do and when to do it . . . you just don't get how hard it is, working . . . hours every day, never feelin' like you're getting somewhere . . . I don't need a woman harping at me when I'm home and finally get a chance to rest."

Suzanne sat very still and then told Jonathan quietly, "And I don't think you realize what it is like to be at home with little ones all day, doing laundry, dishes, and scrubbing floors, just to do it all again the next day. It feels like nothing is ever really finished, it all just keeps repeating and repeating over and over and over again, but . . . I try to be happy when I realize that at least we have a home, unlike many families, and we are keeping our head above water . . . even if it just barely and we have two healthy children and . . ." she faltered, "each other."

Jonathan softened slightly when she said that, "We'll go for a walk and a picnic soon, Suzanne, I promise. Truly, I don't want to disappoint you. It's just been really hard at work lately, lots of tension, lots of pressure to be perfect . . . it gets old after awhile . . . At first, I enjoyed the challenges of working in a restaurant kitchen, but now . . . between the politics of keeping the big brass happy and the complaining customers satisfied and . . . oh, whatever, you're right . . . I realize you work hard too, things will get better, we'll . . . you know, we'll . . ." Jonathan fell asleep before he finished his sentence.

Sitting in the middle of the silence, Suzanne knew she was going to have to tell him soon that she was fairly certain that another baby was on the way. By her calculations, it would be born sometime in late October; and she felt completely undone by the thought of it.

CHAPTER THIRTY-EIGHT

Easter Sunday of 1933, found them all sitting close to the front of the church--Jonathan was wearing his best suit, his only suit, and Suzanne had on her dusky rose dress with the full skirt. She'd let out the belt to hide her slightly expanding figure and buttoned up all the white pearl buttons for a more discreet neckline. As always, her parents, Charles and Grace, looked the very picture of refinement and prosperity, as did her Grandmother and Grandfather Hughes. Grandpa and Grandma Stuart were dressed a little less formally, yet very properly.

Rosie was going to be part of the Easter program and so, everyone had come to church.

Once again, Suzanne marveled at the men in the crowd who were singing out so lustily. Jonathan looked uncomfortable, her father and Grandfather Hughes looked stiff and slightly uncertain while Grandpa Stuart looked rather hot. None of them, however, sang with the congregation.

It was time. Rosie came out on the stage with other children her age that squirmed and pranced nervously about the platform. Rosie immediately came to the fore, ready to do her part. She watched aghast as the other children excitedly worked to find their places. Obviously, she was impatient to begin. When they finally all settled, Rosie stood at attention, looked out at all the people, and demurely started in a very loud voice:

"The whole big world is bright and gay," then she added,

"Oh! I think I have a rock in my shoe" as she held up her brand new white patent leather shoe for all to see.

With a beguiling smile, she finished,

"Do you know why? It's Easter day."

She curtsied, and then returned to her place with the rest of the children while the crowd laughed uproariously as they clapped loudly. Jonathan looked at Suzanne, who looked at Grace, who looked mortified. Grace looked at Grandmother Stuart, who shook her head, smiled and whispered rather loudly, "Don't worry, she's a little child. Everyone is charmed. She did just fine!"

Suzanne relaxed at Grandmother Stuart's word. She turned her attention to the rest of the service, hoping Jonathan would not fall asleep and embarrass them all. Instead, Grandpa Stuart fell asleep. When he started snoring, Grandma Stuart poked him hard in the ribs. Startled, he looked up at the preacher and stayed awake for the rest of the service.

During the next week, Suzanne could not get thoughts of the service out of her mind.

"Early in the morning, He rose from the grave . . . He is not here for He is risen . . . By His stripes, we are healed . . . Jesus said, 'I am the way, the truth, and the life, no man comes to the

Father, but by me' . . . God is love . . . Beloved, He's calling to you . . . He's alive forevermore."

"Time to stop all this pondering," she would think. "The sun is shining, the laundry is waiting, and I've work to do."

As the sunshine returned to Southern California, Suzanne's depression lifted. Spring flowers were blooming all around them and Willow Springs Park was beckoning. Her neighbor, Ann had delivered a baby girl that she named Carol in late December. Now the six of them--Suzanne, Bobby, and Rosie along with Ann, Roger, and baby Carol--would stroll to the park for an afternoon of playtime. Bobby was old enough to join in the fun and baby Carol would sleep, leaving Ann and Suzanne plenty of time to chat. Suzanne's spirit responded to the out-of-doors and the friendship as readily as the trees responded to the sun, creating blossoming new life.

Jonathan joined a baseball team that played in a community league. Suzanne had encouraged him with the idea, hoping it would help his spirits improve. Rosie became the official team mascot. Every Saturday morning the two of them would trot off together--Jonathan in his uniform and Rosie in a tiny replica of his, along with the precious red cowboy boots adorning her feet. Suzanne stayed home, relishing her time with Bobby. After building block forts with him, then singing nursery songs or reading him a book, the two of them would head to the backyard where he loved to play quietly by her side as she sat reading.

Due to her advancing pregnancy, the dancing dates had

to be curtailed; however, Max and Martha invited them over for dinner and cards rather often. The four of them would laugh merrily, playing gin rummy far into the night.

The month of June brought her twenty-third birthday and with it a certain amount of contentment to her spirit. Although she longed for that erstwhile fulfilling relationship with Jonathan, she was finding delight in her children and in her home.

Because of her expanding figure, going out in public was out of the question. Instead, Jonathan tried to make her birthday special by bringing home a cake from the local bakery, then cooking his specialty for dinner--fried chicken, fresh corn on the cob and mashed potatoes. Knowing she would be the one who would have to clean up all that splattered grease and bits of seasoned flour mixed with buttermilk flung all about in her tidy kitchen, Suzanne was not sure she felt particularly pampered. Yet, knowing how hard Jonathan had worked, and how pleased he was with himself, she held her tongue.

After the children went to bed, they sat side by side on the sofa reminiscing.

"Lay your head down and put your feet in my lap," Jonathan told her softly. When she did so, he began gently to rub her swollen feet.

"Honey," he said in a husky voice, "you're the best thing that ever happened to me. I'm a lucky man to have you by my side. We've two healthy children and . . ." he stopped as a sob caught in his throat. She knew he was thinking of Johnny and she stiffened, scared of what was coming next. However, Jonathan patted her shoulder awkwardly and looked down at the swell of her stomach. "And one more coming along," he said, his voice stronger. He stopped again as a faraway look came into his eyes. Then he ended the conversation with something so unexpected, "and ya' know, babies are God's gift of love!"

She remembered when he had said that before Rosie was born. She'd been so shocked by it then and she was shocked by it again. Maybe her tender hearted, charming Jonathan was returning to her. Maybe things were going to be okay for them after all. She went to get ready for bed humming that old favorite of Jonathan's, *Blue Skies*.

CHAPTER THIRTY-NINE

The bustling social and volunteer activities of Grace had slowed for the summer so she would regularly send Ramon to whisk Suzanne and the two children away to the groves for the day. Rosie would dance in glee at the thought of seeing Missy and all of her beloved family members. It soon became apparent that Bobby's favorite was Grandpa Stuart who he followed around as his "G'ndpapa" worked among the groves. His tiny figure could be seen riding along with his grandfather in the cab of the truck or tractor. Suzanne enjoyed catching up on family affairs. At noon, Cook would fix one of her delicious luncheons after which Grandma Stuart or Grace would take charge of the children, leaving Suzanne free to nap or read in the gardens.

Overall, they were lovely days of respite for Suzanne.

It was on such a day that her father joined them for lunch. Though it was a special treat for Suzanne to see her father, she suspected there was a specific reason for the visit. As soon as they finished eating, Charles called Suzanne into the parlor to talk. Trembling, she paced the room, expecting to hear the worst--she feared that Jonathan had been in trouble once more.

Her father started the conversation with, "Dearest, stop fretting, this is not bad news." At which Suzanne sat down at the edge of the settee to listen.

"President Roosevelt has been creating ways for the country to get working again. One of his projects is called the Public Works Administration or PWA for short. The purpose is to employ workers to carry out public works projects such as the construction of public buildings and roads, among other things. The President is working with state and local governments to carry out the project."

Suzanne wondered what all this had to do with her, but she was certain her father would not leave the bank to come home simply to give her a lesson in economics.

"As business leaders in the community, Grandfather Hughes and I have been involved in implementing this program for our city along with the surrounding communities. We could help Jonathan find a job, one where he'd learn a trade and develop a more secure future for your family."

"That sounds very wonderful indeed, father, though I do not understand why you are talking to me about it," Suzanne responded, uncertainty lacing her voice.

"My reasons are two-fold. Jonathan has indicated his desire to be independent and we respect that in him. Additionally, these jobs will potentially be spread all over the State of California which means he would have to travel to them, necessitating being gone from home for long stretches at a time. Of course, the family would gather round to help you out. But, I am concerned for your well being, Suzie girl, especially since you are once again with child."

Feeling rather lightheaded at the sudden proposition, Suzanne sat back on the settee, attempting to gather her thoughts.

"I know it would most likely be rough for you at first, yet it behooves you to consider how likely the work experience Jonathan would gain from these jobs would enable him to find better paying jobs in the future. Again, we will be here to help you out. I have already talked this over with your mother and we have discussed ways to lend you aid during the times Jonathan would be away from home."

In spite of her cumbersome size, Suzanne rose quickly and walked across the room to her father who met her half way. She went into his arms; then laid her head on his shoulder saying sincerely, "Father, thank you. I appreciate that you talked to me first. It has given me time to prepare for it, given me a chance to assimilate the information. I do believe it sounds like a valuable opportunity for our family. I imagine it will be rough, especially with the new baby; but remember, I am still young and we will make it, I'm certain of it." Suzanne kissed his cheek and then added, "I'm feeling rather lightheaded, I believe I'd better lay down now. Let me consider how best to approach Jonathan on this thing. Thank you again, Father. I do love you so."

"And I love you, Suzanne, though I've rarely spoken those words to you. You've been the delight of my life."

He took her hands in his, "I do hope this will be your last child. I fear you will soon be worn out completely if you continue at this rate."

"I know, Father. This was an unexpected surprise. But, Rosie and Bobby are such a joy to me; to us . . . I do love being a mother."

"Of course you do, and we enjoy having them about, especially your mother, though I imagine she will never tell you so. Go, get some rest now, take care of that precious life growing inside of you," Charles remonstrated, as he picked up his hat to leave for the bank.

Lying down upstairs in her former bedroom, which was now a guest bedroom, Suzanne pondered the things her father had said. She feared what would happen if Jonathan were away from home so long, she feared he would start drinking heavily again, she feared his absences would create a chasm between them that could not be crossed, she feared for his safety and also . . . She . . . was so uncertain.

Nevertheless, knowing he was so unhappy in his current job, how could she deny him the opportunity that her father was presenting?

Oh, how she longed to return fully to their former romantic, joyfully intimate times together. They had started to a little bit. Oh, how she wanted those skies of blue Jonathan loved to talk about. Oh, how she longed for those carefree moments when all they thought of was each other. In her heart, Suzanne sleepily acquiesced to this coming change in their lives . . . it was the way it had to be. After all, they would soon have three children to provide for . . . she must think like a woman and not like a starry-eyed girl.

August, 1933
Glendora, California

CHAPTER FORTY

Jonathan's garden yielded a prolific harvest, providing them with peppers, cucumbers, tomatoes, squash, beets, carrots, onions, green beans, lima beans, radishes, cabbages, and even quite a few ears of corn throughout the summer. The apricot tree in the backyard and the fig tree in the front yard each bore fruit in abundance while the wild blackberry bush along the back fence was producing a bountiful crop. Grateful as she was for the bounty, Suzanne had no idea what to do with it all. Her advancing pregnancy and caring for two young children rendered the thought of canning imprudent, to say the least.

Grandmother Stuart heard about her quandary and came over to help. Not to be outdone, Grandmother Hughes sent one of her maids over to lend a hand. A couple of times, Grace came over to help keep Bobby and Rosie from underfoot. Soon rows of Mason jars filled with gleaming jewel toned foodstuffs lined the pantry shelves. Even Rosie got in on the act of turning fresh produce into jars of whole apricots, peeled tomatoes, cut green beans, pickled beets, succotash, sauerkraut, relishes, and a variety of pickles along with several different flavors of jam.

After one particularly laborious day, Grace, Grandma Stuart, and Suzanne were relaxing on the back porch in the Lloyd Loom wicker chairs that once graced Grandfather and Grandmother Hughes' garden. Rosie and Bobby were playing peacefully in the shade of the copious dogwood tree as the ladies sipped Grandpa Stuart's lemonade. Jonathan appeared, starling them all. Suzanne's stomach clenched when she saw him, as his appearance at such times usually heralded bad news.

"Ladies, you are now looking at a WPA man. I've just been given my first assignment. I will be working out of town for three weeks, starting tomorrow. Now aren't ya proud of me!" he exclaimed.

Suzanne started to rise, trying to speak; however, no words came out of her mouth.

"Oh, honey! Don't get up. I know, you're happy and probably a little scared . . . And, maybe wondering about my job at the hotel. With great pleasure, I quit job it, today. That job was shaky anyhow . . . not certain how much longer it would have lasted. Rumor has it, the hotel is closing the restaurant for an extended remodel of the lounge . . . I would've been out of work soon anyway. This is a great opportunity to advance into a steady career. That's what your father said Suzie girl, and he should know."

Emotions tumbled about her as Suzanne sat rooted to the embellished white wicker chair that she had always loved so much. She thought of her father's words regarding the possibility of more security for their family while her thoughts careened with the reality that she'd be home alone with two young children; and that she was seven and half months pregnant!

In the stillness, apparently sensing her concerns, Jonathan continued, "My supervisor knows about your condition. He says that he will make certain that I work close to home when your time comes. And, dearest, your father has promised to get you some help around the house. He said he would make certain you weren't overloaded or lonely while I am away from home. Isn't this just the berries?" Jonathan concluded as he slung his metal lunch pail over his shoulder and headed for the kitchen.

Grace was the first to speak, "Well, I guess that is that. Suzanne, we need to make plans."

As August neared its end, the weather turned exceedingly hot, making Suzanne feel extremely uncomfortable while her expanding frame caused her movements to be ponderous and ungainly. The torrid weather pulled at her strength, leaving her barely able to function.

Fortunately, her father had arranged for the laundry to be taken care of by a washerwoman, her Grandmother Hughes had arranged for a woman to come in and clean once a week, and her mother came by regularly to help with the children. Every few days, Grandmother Stuart sent meals over with Ramon, leaving Suzanne free to rest when the children were napping.

Her neighbor Ann often stopped by to ask if she would like to walk to Willow Springs Park. When she was able, Suzanne would slowly stroll with Ann to the park where Rosie, Bobby, and Roger especially enjoyed splashing merrily in the wading pool. Ann's baby, Carol, was now old enough to sit on her mother's lap to watch and clap her hands in glee at the children's antics.

September came, bringing little relief from the heat. However, as the calendar neared the fall season, a nip settled into the morning air, bringing partial relief to Suzanne. The highlight of Suzanne's week was going to her parent's house for their family Sunday afternoon dinner. Her mother was all for Jonathan's new job with the WPA and thus, bent on being helpful to Suzanne in every way possible. Additionally, Grace seemed so relaxed and peaceful on Sunday afternoons. Suzanne surmised it was the fact that she was going to church on Sunday mornings now. As always, Suzanne could not help but wonder at the changes taking place in her mother life and demeanor.

One such change was the addition of grace being said before they started eating their meal. Grandpa and Grandma Stuart readily complied, as did the uncles and aunts. Grandfather Hughes seemed rather perturbed at being asked to wait for his meal, while Grandmother Hughes appeared uncomfortable. Her cousins, on the other hand, wiggled and sometimes snickered through the prayer. Undaunted, Grace insisted.

It was a wilting Sunday afternoon in mid-September when Rosie asked her grandmother if she could say the grace. Always wanting Rosie to join in her newfound interest in God, Grace readily complied. Rosie bowed her head and recited:

"Over the teeth and past the gums, look out stomach, here it comes."

A deadly silence fell over the table as Rosie looked innocently at her grandmother, expecting praise. Obviously, this was the not the prayer Grace had anticipated and everyone at the table, except Rosie, was aware of her fiery displays of displeasure. Suzanne, feeling overwhelmed with the heat, her pregnancy, and her parental responsibilities could not contain herself. She started to giggle. The harder she tried to stop, the more she giggled. Grandma Stuart soon joined in the merriment. Others began chuckling softly while some of the cousins started laughing right out loud. Even Grandfather Hughes had a tickled look on his face.

"Well, my Rosie girl, where did you learn such a 'prayer'?"

"From my daddy," Rosie answered proudly.

Knowing how Grace carried on about Jonathan's lack of social refinement, the table grew very silent once more.

Finally, Grace broke the silence by patting Rosie's hand and saying, "That was a very special little prayer you said. Now let's thank God for our food then we can eat this delicious dinner that Cook has fixed for us."

Relieved, the family went on to enjoy the rest of the afternoon together.

As each day came and went, Suzanne felt her strength waning; the fatigue was overwhelming. As the chilly weather set in, she developed a cold that soon went into her chest.

Jonathan was working out of town most of the time,

leaving her to sleep alone. She would often dream of sinking into an abyss from which she was unable to climb out to safety. Upon waking, she would be chilled and shaken.

"What is wrong with me?" she worried. "Is my baby going to be okay? Why am I feeling so weak and lightheaded? I need Jonathan," she would cry out to the walls.

Each morning, she would try to be upbeat and cheery for the children's sake, but she felt very alone and ever so frightened by her weakness.

Within a week or two of catching cold, Suzanne began suffering with a cough and experiencing chills along with a fever and headaches. When she developed chest pains, her parents rushed her to Doctor Stevens who immediately put her into the hospital, fearing the worst. Soon Dr. Stevens confirmed that Suzanne had developed pneumonia.

On the 28th day of October with Jonathan called from work to be at her side Suzanne delivered a healthy baby boy, then immediately passed out. Doctor Stevens tried valiantly; however, he was unable to revive her as she slipped into a coma.

CHAPTER FORTY-ONE

The coal-black darkness surrounded her; she began sinking downward, into its depths. She sensed a very great weight on her chest. Feeling overcome, she began to abandon her fight against the darkness, succumbing to its power. As she did, euphoria took over, drawing her toward a radiant light. She saw two small children playing happily together and soon realized it was her Johnny and little Dan. The peace was palpable; the boys appeared unencumbered and serene. She moved toward them, but a barrier lay before her, a barrier she could not seem to cross.

Suzanne struggled forward. Oh! How she wanted to see Johnny, to touch his face, feel his warm breath on her cheek, cuddle him in her arms once more. The barrier was stopping her, as was something else. Though now floating weightless in the darkness, an urgent voice was calling her back to the place she had just left. The voice was familiar, yet eerily disjointed and distant,

"Suzie girl . . . you must come back to us . . . children need you . . . and Jonathan . . . we want you to live . . ."

"Live?" Suzanne pondered. She was alive, she had just seen Johnny and she wanted to join him, but that barrier . . . she was . . . trying to . . .

She heard a loud, piercing cry that pulled hard at her; she was about to resist, preferring to keep on with her quest towards Johnny, when a third voice was added,

"Mama, mama, why won't you talk to me, mama? Sing me a song . . . tell me a story . . . I want a kiss, mama. I'll sing you a song . . . 'Jesus loves me' . . . ," the voice faded and Suzanne moved once again toward Johnny.

Another voice, ragged with pain pleaded,

"Darling Suzanne, don't die . . . I can't live without you . . . I'd be lost forever . . . I . . ."

Then the very familiar voice added,

"Think of Rosie . . . Bobby . . . and your baby . . . Fight . . . breathe . . . live, you've got to live, Suzie girl!"

The weight came down hard on her chest . . . the darkness was . . . so hard to . . . fight against and she was . . . not sure of what . . . to do . . . she wanted to go to Johnny, but the voices and there was . . . that crying. It was her baby, but it was not baby Johnny . . . it was . . .

Her eyes fluttered and her body convulsed with pain as she struggled to breathe. Through a haze of fatigue, she saw faces . . . her father, Jonathan, her mother . . . Rosie . . . Rosie . . . She needed to take care of Rosie and where was Bobby and . . . there was something else, a baby . . . she started to rise, but she could not . . . She was . . . it was . . . so hard . . .

Suzanne coughed violently, and then looked toward

Jonathan who cried out, "You woke up!"

Unable to speak, Suzanne began to cry softly.

An oxygen tent was erected around her bed, keeping her loved ones from reaching her. However, their faces held her gaze as they crumpled into joyful smiles of relief. Her mother's head was bowed in humble submission, making Suzanne wonder once more at the changes she had beheld in her mother.

Her father ran out, presumably to find the doctor while, as usual, Rosie was dancing about in delight. Jonathan, looking extremely disheveled, could hardly contain himself, his entire being was charged with excitement. Suzanne knew him well enough to realize he was just barely holding back from ripping open the tent to grab her and kiss her. Fortunately, he refrained from doing so.

Unaware of all that had transpired during the long days following the baby's birth, Suzanne weakly spoke, "Hi, everyone. You all seem so happy."

Her mother stepped forward, "My dear, you have been battling severe pneumonia. We thought and actually the doctor was certain, that you were going to die."

In a voice shaking with fear, awe, and relief mixed together randomly, Grace continued, "God has answered my prayers. He has brought you through this! Suzanne, we are ever so grateful that you have come back to us."

Rosie interposed, "I love's you mama dear!"

Causing Suzanne to ask, "Where is my little Bobby?"

And, then she struggled to look down at her stomach, "The baby, what's happened, where is it?" Then in a panic filled voice, she inquired shakily, "Did it die?"

"No," her mother replied. "You delivered the baby, a healthy little boy, and then passed out. You have been that way for the past several days. The nursing staff has been caring for him. They brought him in a couple of times and held him up near you, hoping you would sense his presence and respond to it. He was here, just a few minutes ago; he started to cry, so they took him for a feeding. Grandpa and Grandma Stuart have been taking care of Bobby. Doctor Stevens had us bring Rosie in to see you. It was a last attempt to rouse you."

"I heard Rosie and . . . a baby crying . . . and daddy, I heard him talking and . . . I heard Jonathan, too . . . oh, mother, I saw Johnny, he was playing with little Dan and they were . . . oh, he must have been in Heaven, I guess. I was trying to reach . . . oh my goodness, I was going to, but now . . . I'm awfully tired . . ."

Dr. Stevens came in followed by her father. "Well, young lady. I am very happy to see you are awake. However, you must rest now. It is imperative that you not overtax yourself. Family, I know you are overjoyed and want to visit with Suzanne, but she must not wear herself out. You can come back to see her this evening, if she continues to improve."

As silence fell over the room, Suzanne began to understand how close she'd come to death. In spite of her intense desire to see Johnny, to hold him again, she wanted, far more, to live--for Rosie, for Bobby, for the new baby boy . . . who did not even have a name yet . . . "little baby with no name," she thought as a giddy giggle rose out of her being. "And for Jonathan," she knew, she wanted to live for her dearest Jonathan.

CHAPTER FORTY-TWO

After everyone left and she was alone in the quiet, Suzanne pondered her mother's words, "God answered my prayers; He's brought you through this."

Ever since baby Johnny's funeral, she'd wondered about God, about what happens to people when they die, and about Molly telling her that Johnny was in Heaven. The words of that preacher came back to her once more, "Because I live, you will live also . . . I am the resurrection and the life. He who believes in Me, though he may die, he will live. Whoever lives and believes in Me will never die. If you know the Savior, if you have accepted the sacrifice he made for you at Calvary, you will see Johnny again in Heaven."

She realized now that she had nearly died, and she had seen Johnny, she was certain of it. He was in Heaven; she was certain of that also. However, there had been a barrier she could not cross, of that she was also certain. Yet, she had no understanding of the barrier; she was baffled by it . . . as much as she was baffled by those words of the preacher that she had never been able to get out of her mind. And, she longed so to understand more.

Steadily regaining strength, Suzanne was soon able to sit up. The momentous day came when she could actually hold her new baby. She gazed into his little face and she loved him just as much as she had loved the others. Her heart swelled with emotion and she was grateful that she was alive to care for this little one. This would be her last baby. Dr. Stevens had told them both sternly that another baby might kill her; she simply could not risk having any more children.

After some deliberation, they had decided on the name William Edward for the baby--William for Jonathan's father and Edward for her brother. They would call him little Willie.

Returning from a walk along the corridor, Suzanne saw a man sitting in her room. As she came closer, she realized it was the pastor from her mother's church. Suzanne allowed the nurse to help her back into bed, and then asked curiously, "Why did you come to see me? Is everything all right with my mother?"

The pastor responded with a smile, "Your mother is just fine. We are so pleased to have her as part of our congregation. I came to visit because your mother explained to me the gravity of your recent illness. She told me of her prayers for you, and about your miraculous recovery. It has been such sustenance for her faith. "

"Oh, I see," Suzanne replied, though she did not really understand his comment about faith.

"I imagine your ordeal was rather frightening."

"It was," Suzanne answered quietly, wondering if she

should tell him about seeing baby Johnny. He might know about the barrier. But, she hardly knew him, she had never actually talked with him before, and she was rather uncertain how he would react to such a story.

She decided to continue, "I felt such darkness, it was pulling me under, then I saw this brilliant light," she hesitated . . .

"Please go on. I've talked with others who've encountered such an occurrence."

"I saw my baby, my baby Johnny; he died, from crib death, when he was an infant. He was playing with his cousin, who died the same way. It felt so peaceful, they were so content . . . I wanted to go to them. However, I could not because a barrier stood in the way. It was not something that I could see, I just knew it was there and that I could not go past it."

Speaking very gently, the pastor asked, "Suzanne, have you settled your soul with the Savior?"

Having no idea what he was talking about, she had no idea how to answer him. Apparently sensing her confusion, this time he asked, "Suzanne, have you asked the Lord Jesus Christ to become the master of your soul . . . asked him to forgive . . . ,"

"I don't really know about Jesus, I've certainly never talked to Him . . . how does one do that? My mother said she'd prayed to God about me, but . . . I am unsure of . . ."

"I'd be happy to tell you more, show you from the Bible how to know about Jesus."

As she considered his offer, she thought about Jonathan.

She doubted he would like her looking into this, he usually got angry when her mother even mentioned going to church. He had gone on that Easter Sunday to see Rosie. Nevertheless, he had been extremely grumpy and difficult afterwards. She supposed she should just tell this man thank you for coming and send him on his way. Yet, her heart was tugging her forward. She really wanted to know more and she certainly wanted to understand about the barrier.

"Okay," Suzanne spoke cautiously, "you can tell me more. First though, I want to understand about the barrier, I want to know why I could not pass it."

Taking a deep breath, the pastor began, "Heaven is God's dwelling place. God is holy and because He is holy, He cannot allow anything unclean, such as sin, into His presence and all of us, every man or woman born on this earth, commits sin at some point in our lives. Although we are His beloved creation, our sin has created a barrier between God and us. Unless that sin has been forgiven by Jesus Christ, the barrier cannot be crossed."

"I see, well, I think that I do," Suzanne responded thoughtfully. "I know that I have sinned, I can have an awfully bad temper sometimes, it's gotten me into trouble before, especially with my mother and sometimes with my husband and sometimes I hate people so much, like my husband's mother, she's a mean old lady who causes trouble for everyone and then . . ."

The pastor stopped her, "The important thing is, God provided a way past the barrier. That way is through Jesus Christ.

He took God's punishment for our sins when He died on the cross. If we ask Him, He willingly covers or forgives our sins and the barrier between God and us is then removed. However, each individual person must accept Jesus' offer to cover those sins." The pastor took his Bible and showed her where in it these things were written. Suzanne listened with rapt attention.

CHAPTER FORTY-THREE

For a long while after the pastor had gone, Suzanne considered his words. Something was pulling at her, urging her along toward a resolution of the issue. She was convinced that Johnny was alive; certain he was in the place people called Heaven. In her heart, she knew it was true--those things the pastor said, then showed her written in the Bible.

The pastor called the Bible, "God's Word." He read to her from pages in it that he called the book of Romans. He explained that God had men write down His words so that people could understand who He is and why Jesus came to live on the earth as a baby who grew into a man. It was so people could see what God was like. He told her Jesus had lived a perfect life, exactly how God wants all men to live.

"Nevertheless," he'd said, "Jesus, who himself never sinned, chose to die at the cross in order to take God's punishment for the sins of all mankind."

She had been so entranced by what the pastor was saying that she had not even asked his name. In retrospect, it seemed so rude; she wished she knew his name. She longed to talk with him more. When he had realized that she was growing tired, he gently said good-bye. He left a Bible with her so she could read it for herself, read more about the things they had been discussing. He told her that the book of John would tell her more about Jesus.

The last thing the pastor had told her was that accepting Jesus' offer of forgiveness brought peace to a person that was beyond explanation or understanding. He asked if he could pray with her and she had said, "Yes." In his prayer, he requested that God help Suzanne find peace everlasting for her soul. That sounded wondrous, she had always felt so restless inside, she longed for peacefulness that did not leave her, even when life got muddled and painful.

Suzanne struggled against the fatigue that was mercilessly yanking her toward sleep. Her mind could not assimilate anymore; her body would not stay awake any longer. She yielded and slept for several hours. When she woke, her mother was sitting next to the bed, holding her hand, with her head bowed, apparently in prayer.

"Mother, are you praying?" Suzanne asked.

"Yes, Suzanne, I am. Praying for you, praying that you will soon be well enough to go home, praying that you will come to know Jesus as I have. It is the most marvelous thing that has ever happened to me, it has brought me such peace."

"I am thinking about it, Mother. A pastor from your church came here earlier. He talked to me, talked to me about peace. He showed me things from the Bible . . . left me one to read, it is right over there," Suzanne said, pointing to the table by her bed. "I have been mulling over what he said, but I need more time to consider what it all means for my life . . . that is, my life and Jonathan's."

Uncharacteristically, her mother merely said, "I understand. I do not want to push you. I will just keep praying. Please, though, won't you tell me if you want to talk some more about it?"

"I will, Mother, I certainly will. How are Rosie and Bobby doing today? I miss them so very much."

"Jonathan took them to play at the park. They were over the moon with joy about it!"

"That is wonderful to hear. Thank you so very much for taking such good care of everything while I've been so ill."

"Certainly, my dear, I am sure that you realize how much your father has done for you and . . ."

"I do, mother, please tell him what I said," Suzanne added hastily.

"I think I should go now and let you rest."

Gazing out the window at the vivid sunshine and the autumn trees, which still bore a smattering of their leaves burnished plum, saffron, and fiery orange, Suzanne thought of Nathaniel Hawthorne's comment about the season ~

I cannot endure to waste anything as precious as autumn sunshine by staying in the house.

"Oh, mother, I am so sick of resting. I just woke up from a long nap. I want to get up, go outside, do things again . . . be with my children. I've hardly seen little Willie. I know the hospital staff is taking good care of him, but I want to go home and take care of him myself . . . be with Jonathan."

"Well, you must be getting well, that is a good sign. I will make certain Doctor Stevens knows about this restlessness of yours, maybe he will be inclined to send you home sooner," Grace stated hopefully as she leaned over to give Suzanne a kiss on the cheek.

Alone once more, Suzanne knew exactly what she wanted to do. Quietly, in hesitating words, she asked Jesus to become part of her life. It all seemed so simple. Yet, at that very moment, peace that was indescribable flooded her soul. Suzanne knew her life had changed forever; and she realized that the change would bring much good to her.

CHAPTER FORTY-FOUR

The reds and the greens, the golds and the silvers sparkled throughout the merry season of Christmas helping Suzanne back to full health in body and spirit. She had always loved the month of December. Rosie turned four years old on December 2nd, Bobby was growing apace, little Willie was thriving, and she was ever so grateful to be alive.

For their fifth anniversary, Jonathan took her out to dinner, then to the Pasadena Playhouse where they saw a play written by George Bernard Shaw called *Too Good to Be Good.* They had not been back to the Playhouse since Uncle Gerard treated them before Rosie was born. All three children stayed the night with her parents. It was heavenly to be out alone with Jonathan once more, especially when half way through the play he whispered in her ear, "Honey, you're still the most beautiful girl in the room."

Suzanne was filled with amazement at the changes taking place in her heart. She found herself more patient with the children's busyness as well as more tolerant of the differences between herself and Jonathan. She fretted far less, and no longer felt such empty places lingering in her heart.

Grace went all out to make their Christmas an especially spectacular one. She told anyone who would listen, "Our family has much to celebrate this year."

With President Roosevelt at the helm, the economic depression seemed to be loosening its grip on the nation.

The Eighteenth Amendment establishing Prohibition was repealed by passage of the Twenty-First Amendment, relieving Suzanne of the worry that Jonathan would be arrested again at a speakeasy. Though he was often out of town working, his job provided enough money to pay their expenses with some left over for an emergency savings account. So far, Jonathan had arrived home from each trip in good spirits, and fully sober. When Jonathan was home, they would occasionally take in a movie or spend the evening playing cards with Max and Martha.

Life settled once more into a predictable pattern of work woven through with pleasant joys. Suzanne's newfound faith was still her very own secret; she had yet to share it with her mother. She did not want her mother's forceful nature to override her own quest to understand things for herself. Whenever she was alone, once the children were in bed for the evening, she read the Bible with a profound hunger for more knowledge. Jonathan still had no idea of the changes taking place in her soul.

With more peace than ever before, Suzanne traversed the very rainy winter season of 1934. Though she still felt the searing loss as the third anniversary of baby Johnny's death drew near, Suzanne met the challenge with the help of her newfound Savior.

Once more pondering the words said by the preacher on that dark, gloomy day she was comforted with the assurance that she would indeed see baby Johnny again, in Heaven some day. Amazement gripped her heart as she realized anew how precious was her salvation.

It was time to tell her mother, she had put it off far too long. Not trusting herself to speak without an avalanche of tears, Suzanne decided to convey the news to her mother in a letter. She wrote:

April 3, 1934

Dearest Mother,

If you are not sitting down, you should do so as I imagine the contents of this letter will bring you a tremendous surprise.

No, it is not another baby. However, you will be overjoyed with my news.

I have chosen to follow Jesus, as you have been praying I would do. Your pastor left a Bible when he visited me in the hospital. I have been reading it, and I've found it a captivating book. I especially like to read in the Psalms, though I love learning more about Jesus in the book of John.

I have not told Jonathan about this yet as I am not at all sure how he will take the news. As you know, certain things can make him most upset. So for right now, I would rather keep this between you and me. I know you will understand.

The anniversary of baby Johnny's death and the date of his funeral were easier to get through this year, because now I know that Johnny is in Heaven and that I will see him again someday. Next time Jonathan is away, I would really like to come with the children to attend church with you.

Your loving daughter,
Suzanne

After she mailed the letter, Suzanne experienced such relief--it felt wonderful to have told someone her exciting news at last.

Just as she had anticipated, the moment her mother read the letter, Grace headed right over to see Suzanne.

With tears in her eyes, Grace held on to Suzanne's hands and together they said a prayer of thanksgiving.

CHAPTER FORTY-FIVE

Springtime burst into action abounding with multiple earthly delights. Tending to her thriving brood, Suzanne thought of Molly's words about May: "Tis a grand month, it is . . . with all the flowers bloomin'. . . bluebirds soarin' . . . and the weather balmy. Why, the air's so thick with the goodness of life that you can feel it swirlin' around 'ya . . . and, spreadin' all throughout your very soul."

She missed Molly so much, wondering often how she was doing over in Ireland and if she had found peace for her aching heart. Suzanne wished she could share her newfound faith with Molly, wished she could hug her once more, wished they could spend time chatting together. Oh, how grand it would be to tell her about glimpsing Johnny and little Dan playing together in Heaven.

June would bring her 24th birthday and Suzanne could hardly believe she could be that old. Nor could she believe that they were already almost half way through the year 1934. Though there were occasional days when she still longed for more freedom and the fulfillment of her dreams about traveling the world as a journalist, Suzanne felt more contented, undeniably more at peace than she ever thought possible. The churning restlessness she often experienced previously had abated, leaving in its wake a strong desire to persevere in the life she had chosen for herself.

She had chosen this life on that day when she left home with Jonathan to marry in such haste. Now, as a mother to three children, she was going to make a happy life for them. They would play baseball and see movies, go fishing and camping, take part in Girl Scouts and Boy Scouts, participate in county fairs and barn dances, make good friends and love their family, they would sing and laugh and cry together--Suzanne determined to be a mother who was involved with her children and the things that interested them. She simply was not going to be the same frenetic force as her mother who, until recently, had never really been one to embrace or enjoy her family.

It was time to dance again. Suzanne felt the desire for it surging through her; she hoped Jonathan felt the same way. He was away on another job assignment, but when he came home, she would bring it up to him. In the meantime, she had the radio as well as the upright player piano her family had given them for Christmas. Music brought her heart such solace along with so much delight. She would run her hands over the keys as she went about her household tasks, she would try to peck out a tune or two when she had a free moment, and when all three children napped at the same time, and she would close their bedroom doors and put a roll in the box above the keyboard. As the piano pinged out Scott Joplin playing the *Maple Leaf Rag* or *The Entertainer*, she would dance with wild abandon.

Those Sundays when Jonathan was out of town, she was able to attend church with her mother. While there, she would bask in the music and listen intently to the sermon. The week following, Suzanne would find herself humming snatches of the songs she'd heard, bringing serenity into the busyness of her days. It was an entirely new sensation to sing aloud of her feelings about God and His wondrous works. She also kept reading in her Bible; she especially related to the Psalms and the way David expressed his thoughts about the extremities of life.

It was a perfectly spectacular summer day in early July. Rosie was staying with her mother, Bobby was "helping" Grandpa Stuart, and Willie was napping. Suzanne took the opportunity to clear out some boxes that had been shoved to the back of the hall closet for far too long. She came upon the costume her mother had made for her to attend the Masque of the Yellow Moon in high school. She slipped on the pink organza, off-the-shoulder dress.

Amazingly, it still fit her perfectly.

The wide skirt reached clear to the floor and the bottom of it. The skirt was embellished with four tiers of ruffles, and delicate organza roses in pastel shades circled the waist and cascaded in rows down the front. Matching roses adorned the shoulders and fluttered across the top of the bust. The wide brim of the white silk hat was circled with pink satin ribbon while a trail of organza roses cascaded down the back. The entire ensemble was breathtaking!

As she twirled, the full skirt swished over the wooden floor, flooding her mind with memories of that high school dance along with the many boys whose names had filled her dance card. Back then, life had been filled with society events and schoolwork along with tennis and typing articles for the school newspaper. She had been so anxious to break free of it all, never realizing how simple and carefree life had been then. Yet, she'd been but a callow youth, filled with thoughts of herself and little else. She only knew people who were like her and her family. Jonathan had showed her that there was so much more to life. He had taught her how to have fun, to laugh, and to sing as well as to embrace diversity instead of shunning it.

She realized now, what a narrow view she once had about people. Her mother had such impossibly high standards that few measured up and fewer still stayed in her good graces. Coming to realize that it was variety in people that made the world a fascinating place also made her realize that their differences did not make them wrong. She had grown to embrace Jonathan's idiosyncrasies. She knew they were the things that made him so interesting to be around--his humor, his delight in people's individuality, his willingness to try out new things, his unorthodox approach to solving problems, and his intense thirst for knowledge. Though he irritated her at times, she actually had grown to cherish his unusual ways; he was fascinating and fun.

Over these years, life had brought her ecstatic joys along with harsh realities. There had been times when she was certain her heart was so broken it could never be right again. Still, it was through the difficult times that she had become stronger as well as more sure of herself. Most of all, she'd learned more about God's love for her and about Jesus, causing an amazing change in her life, one that she was just beginning to understand.

Reflectively, Suzanne mused, "I am not that girl any more. I was looking for a life filled with romantic moments like those that I saw in the movies, one that revolved around my own ideals and my petty whims. Instead, I found out that love has to be strong, that it is more about giving and adapting than about moonlight and dancing. I have become a mother and found the joy of cherishing my children as well as my family. I have survived painful hardships and found I could keep on living."

On that day, Suzanne determined that she would find fulfillment in her family, in her faith, and from within her own circumstances, instead of constantly longing for something else more fulfilling out there in the great misty beyond.

"I guess I've become a woman," she thought. "And, I rather like it."

Before she took the dress off to pack it away again, Jonathan unexpectedly appeared in the doorway. He whistled in appreciation and swept her into a captivating embrace.

"It's time you and I went out dancing again, my dearest!"

Giggling with delight, Suzanne reveled in the moment, secretly hoping that Willie would take a nice long nap.

September, 1934
Glendora, California

CHAPTER FORTY-SIX

Apparently, Maggie Mae was quite ill with some type of mysterious ailment. Jonathan went to see her at least once a week, often taking Rosie with him. Suzanne just could not go near that house. Further, she was uneasy about Bobby being around Maggie Mae, even with Jonathan present. She was not quite sure why, she just did not want him there. Willie was still too young for such a visit. Consequently, Jonathan and Rosie went to bring comfort and tend to Maggie Mae's needs.

Rosie thrived on an audience, and she knew grandmamma Maggie reveled in her antics. Singing from her large repertoire of beloved songs, dancing in her comical way, or delivering a hodgepodge soliloquy, Rosie could light up a room with her whimsical charms. Their neighbor, Ann, was certain she was as talented as Shirley Temple was and felt that Rosie "ought to be in pictures, too!"

However, Suzanne had never seen a Shirley Temple movie; Jonathan simply was not interested. Neither of them took Ann's comments seriously.

Danny came from Arizona to see his mother a time or two. Each trip, he would stop by to visit their family before he returned home. He did not seem overly concerned about his mother. He would always say to Jonathan dryly, "You know, she's always been somewhat of a hypochondriac, rather overly dramatic about things, in my opinion."

Suzanne was distressed to see Danny looking haggard and weary, his actions unsteady, and his speech disjointed. It appeared he was living the life of a hermit, working with Uncle Gerard and doing little else but drinking himself senseless. He did not mention Molly and, Suzanne felt it best to leave the subject alone.

It was well past midnight in late September when Maggie Mae telephoned Jonathan for help. Wearily he told her, "Ma, can't it wait till morning? I just barely got to bed, worked late tonight. Are you dyin' or somethin'? Go back to sleep. We'll talk in the morning."

In spite of her intense dislike of Maggie Mae, Suzanne felt his attitude rather harsh.

"Jonathan, she's never called you this late at night, maybe something is really wrong. Maybe you'd better drive out there to see her."

Disgruntled, Jonathan threw on some clothes and strode out of the house, slamming the door on his way out. Fortunately, the children slept through it all.

Feeling very unsure of herself, Suzanne prayed, using words she'd heard others use, "Lord, please keep Jonathan safe, he's tired, and be with Maggie Mae, too. In spite of her mean ways and her dreadful choices, she needs Your love . . . she needs, she needs something Lord, please keep them in your care."

Though she tried valiantly to fall back asleep, she could not. Deep down, Suzanne felt something was terribly amiss; and, Jonathan still had not returned. Just as the rosy tints of dawn streaked across the sky, Suzanne fell into a fitful sleep.

Asleep for barely an hour, Suzanne woke to find Jonathan sitting at the side of their bed holding his head between his hands. She realized he was crying and, for a moment, did not know what to say or do.

"Jonathan, what's happened?" she finally ventured.

"She's gone," he replied in a hoarse voice. "Just like that . . . she thrashed around and muttered, 'it's too late,' then she started to breathe funny . . . it sounded like a baby's rattle . . . her face, it twisted up horribly . . . and then she was still. She's dead, my mother is dead."

Shaking and sweating, Jonathan gripped the bedpost.

"Oh!" was all that came out of Suzanne's mouth. She felt so uncertain.

"Honey, I am sorry. It must have been terrible for you."

"It was. Danny did not even get to say good-bye. We didn't know she was dying. She is not old enough to die. I'm glad Rosie wasn't there to see it, how awful it could have been for her. What if I hadn't gone over there, Suzanne?"

Suzanne waited.

Jonathan continued, his voice apologetic, "I know, I slammed the door on my way out, I was rude and rough and so very wrong. I am afraid, Suzanne. Maybe this family is cursed like Molly said, maybe . . ."

"Nonsense," Suzanne replied forcefully. "I do not believe that. We've three healthy children, my whole family is alive and well, we are young and strong. Your mother . . . Jonathan, you know that she, well . . . you've got to know that her lifestyle was . . . she lived a rough life, and . . ."

"You don't need to say anymore. The doctor said the same thing in a vague sort of way. It's just that . . . I feel lost, I'm . . ."

Moaning, Jonathan could not finish his thought.

"You needn't say any more about it unless you would like to. I am aware life has been very demanding for you lately. I know it has worn you out . . . working out of town, going to see your mother, taking care of things around here . . . I understand you have had some hard days, I'm sorry for you about that. Nevertheless, no more talk about this family being cursed. I do not ever want you to say such in thing in front the children, especially Rosie; she would pick that right up and ask lots of questions, she is too young to hear such comments. Grieve all you need to, but you must buck up in front of the kids. I need your promise on that, Jon! I mean it; you must do this for our children."

"Of course, of course, I don't want to hurt Rosie or Bobby or little Willie. I know, I understand, I won't . . . you have my word."

Tenderly, Suzanne put her arm around Jonathan's heaving shoulders. She had never seen him like this and felt so ill equipped to meet such a crisis.

"Jonathan, you know that God . . ."

"Don't want to hear about God, that stuff is for old women and children."

"No, that's not true. He's for everyone, I've been learning about His love from my mother and . . ."

"I don't want to hear any more, I said. I was wrong to be angry before, but don't push me . . . 'cause I might lose my temper again. I don't want to do that . . . so, just stop, no more about this God business!"

"Okay, I . . . I won't. I do love you and I . . . Let's go make the coffee and start breakfast, the baby will be up soon, then Rosie and Bobby. We need to pull ourselves together before Rosie's up and asking questions, if she gets upset, then so will Bobby and . . ."

Wearily pulling himself upright, Jonathan followed Suzanne into the kitchen. It was going to be a very long day; she needed all the help she could find. She would call her father and mother later. Right now, though, she whispered a little prayer,

"I'm so new at this, Jesus. Help me. I am afraid. Show me what to do to help Jonathan."

As Suzanne prepared Jonathan a mug of coffee, she added two spoonfuls of their precious sugar, hoping he would sense her love through the small gesture. Maybe later, when Jonathan was gone to work, she would talk to the pastor at her mother's church about these things. For now, though, she was pleasantly surprised at how quickly her heart calmed down and how peaceful she felt immediately after she finished praying.

Then she added, "Thank you, Jesus, I'm doing better now . . . Oh, I guess I am supposed to say amen so you know I'm finished . . . uh, amen."

Sitting side by side on the davenport, Jonathan with his coffee and Suzanne with her tea, they began to plan a funeral for Maggie Mae.

October, 1934
Glendora, California

CHAPTER FORTY-SEVEN

Jonathan knelt by his mother's grave with head down, his shoulders drooping in abject misery. Suzanne stood back, allowing him time alone to say his good-byes.

As she waited, Suzanne gazed at the sky overhead. Brilliant hues of blue from azure to sapphire to cerulean peeked out from clouds shaped like Trojan horses and humpback whales. The October sun cast a golden haze over everything, making it appear to be a bountiful day graced by autumnal delights.

Suzanne's curiosity was piqued; Jonathan and his mother had spent so little time together over the past few years. "What's going on?" she wondered. Surely, he wasn't feeling guilty. After all, if there was a rift, Maggie Mae had caused it. She was a hard, repugnant woman. And, with such vile comments constantly coming out of her mouth, it was understandable that he'd wanted to shun her presence. It seemed little Rosie was the only creature alive who had escaped her foul ways.

She walked toward Jonathan, pondering. "What's making Jon so full of torment today?" she spoke, not realizing she had said it aloud. Startled by the sound of her own voice, she feared Jonathan might have heard. She was relieved when he did not appear to notice.

Feeling as though he might need her support, Suzanne moved closer and finally came to stand alongside Jonathan silently, so as not to disturb his grief.

He was speaking, talking out loud toward the grave, "Ma, why . . . why'd you do it? How could you? Your own grandsons, your own flesh and blood, my boy . . . named after me, and little Dan, named after Danny . . . why'd you do it? How could you, I don't understand, why . . . what made you think you could get away with such a horrendous . . ."

Jonathan looked up with a start when he realized that Suzanne was standing beside him.

As he stood up, he said, "I . . . um, it's um . . ."

"Jonathan, were you just talking to your mother? She cannot hear you, why are you talking to her? What were you saying?"

Suzanne stopped, uncertain of what to say next. She hated to upset Jonathan at such a time. Yet, it sounded like . . . he'd used the word horrendous and . . . he said . . .

"Jonathan, what were you saying about baby Johnny and little Dan?"

"Nothing, it's nothing at all, just calm down."

"I am calm Jonathan. However, I can see how very upset you are. What is going on, what were you saying? You look like you've seen a ghost or something."

At the word "ghost," Jonathan blanched, then spat out the words, "My mother," with such venom that Suzanne reeled at the sound, "my mother said . . . she . . . she said, that . . . Oh! It's just too hard to say it. I can't."

"Jonathan, what is it, what is too hard to say?"

Suzanne froze as suspicion began dawning in her mind. Oh, how she hoped it was not so; such a thought was impossible . . . she could not grasp it; yet, with a flash of understanding, Suzanne knew. The world started to revolve as a thick darkness began closing in around her.

Trembling with fear, anger, sorrow, and unbelief, Suzanne spoke in barely a whisper, "Jonathan, I'm feeling faint . . . I, think I am going to be sick, I . . . ."

Taking a deep breath, Jonathan pulled Suzanne close, steadying her. Then, he slumped again, and put his face down into her lovely auburn hair that fell around her shoulders in soft waves. He started to sob and the sound was piercing, like the cry of a badly wounded animal. For several moments, Jonathan cried, unable to speak.

Suzanne waited silently, fighting to stay upright and in control of her own emotions.

Hoarsely, Jonathan finally spoke, "We've got to get out of here. I can't say it, not here, in the place where . . . not right here."

"I understand, Jonathan. Let's just walk a little, find a bench or something, you're in no shape to drive right now."

Mutely, Jonathan followed her lead as she walked up a slight incline toward the warmth of the sunshine. Suzanne walked fast. She wanted to get them away from the aura of Maggie Mae, the freshly dug grave, and the reality that was bursting inside her chest.

CHAPTER FORTY-EIGHT

Though the sun was warm, Suzanne shivered as they sat on the small wooden bench she found on the top of a small knoll.

"It's time to tell me, Jonathan. You need to tell me what's happened."

"That awful night," he began slowly, "the night when my mother called me to come . . . she knew that she was dying. When I got there, she pulled me close to her and said, 'I've got somethin to tell ya' Patrick, it was me that killed that baby of yer's, he was scrawny and ugly . . . He wasn't fit to live, nor fit to carry on yer name. I smothered him . . . smothered him with that silly little pillow that had *Jonathan Patrick* embroidered on it. That is your name . . . he didn't deserve to have your name. He was an ugly, ugly baby.'"

Suzanne sucked in her breath, and then collapsed against Jonathan as he continued, "I was so taken aback . . . I couldn't speak. Finally, I said, 'How could you Mother?' and then, she laughed and said, 'It was easy . . . and easier with that boy that belonged to Danny and Maggie. . . that brat wasn't fit to bear Danny's name . . . couldn't stand him . . . or that Molly . . . I say, it was good riddance when she left.' My mother actually said those words, Suzanne! Isn't it the most revolting thing you've heard of, ever in your whole life?"

Violently shuddering, Suzanne could only nod.

"My dearest Suzy," Jonathan said in a voice trembling with grief and fear. Stroking her hair he went on, "I don't know what to say to you. It is far too much to bear, my own mother, her own grandsons, her own flesh and blood. How could she? . . . Why did she? . . . I loved Johnny so . . . and then . . . there is the matter of little Dan, how could she do that to Danny and Molly? She drove Molly away, destroying their marriage with her evil actions. How could she do it? My mother . . . my own mother! Oh, Suzanne," he cried out brokenly.

Malevolent rage rose in Suzanne's heart, rage that sped toward her throat with acerbic bile, like a billowing ocean looking for escape from its confines. That horrible, old, deranged woman! Suzanne knew that if the appalling bile spilled out, she would regret the explosion and the harm it would bring. If released, it would spill out all over the plush verdant grass, all over Jonathan, all over their life.

Suzanne worked to gain control of herself as the wrath began to seep out her very pores.

Within herself, she reasoned. "It is not Jonathan's fault; he is overcome with grief about all this. Obviously, he's feeling the loss of baby Johnny and little Dan all over again."

She had to stop the storm that was pulsating through her,

threatening to spill out of her mouth. Nevertheless, like a mighty force it was rising!

Suzanne tried to reign in her fury, yet felt helpless against it. Quite suddenly, she realized what she needed to do. So she prayed,

"Jesus, this is unbearable news, but I can't hurt Jonathan any further with my anger when he is suffering so. I desperately need your help. Right now . . . please!"

At that moment, peace, that was inexplicable, washed over her, soothing the torment that was threatening to overcome her reason.

Calmly, Suzanne spoke, "I cannot imagine what you are feeling right now. Your mother's acts were despicable--they were beyond belief. Whatever drove her to do what she did, it is not because of you or anything you did. You must realize that, you must believe and rely on it or you will be defeated by it."

Jonathan began to shake uncontrollably as Suzanne continued, "We cannot allow her to keep us hostage to the evil she's thrust upon us, and we must not let her win with this thing. . . Jonathan, we need to pull together now. We must choose to live our lives well . . . for our three living children. Baby Johnny is in heaven, I know he is, and he's safe there. We are all safer now that your mother is gone. She has gone to her maker, Jonathan. God will mete out her judgment."

He looked at Suzanne with love flowing from his eyes, a love that had matured over the years, a love that had grown even in these past few minutes.

"I wasn't sure what you'd think or do, I thought maybe you would take the children and leave, maybe you'd never want to see me again, I . . . I couldn't face life without you, without our children . . . I love you, Suzy girl, you are the best thing that ever happened to me."

As the shaking subsided, he continued, "Thank you for what you said . . . I . . . it's so appalling to find this out about my own mother, she's . . . she was . . . that's crazy . . . she was a criminal . . . it was murder, she killed her own grandson, our baby Johnny, our boy . . . and I hate her, I hate for the horrendous things she did in her life, the choices she made . . . and the way she lived. And, I especially can't bear to think about what she did to our baby Johnny and little Dan."

"I know Jon, they were unspeakable things she did. You've a good reason to feel that way. Nonetheless, we cannot allow that spirit of evil and fear and distrust into our lives or it will destroy us all."

Jonathan nodded mutely as Suzanne continued, "Together, we will make a happy life for our children . . . we will, I am determined and you must be too, you must. Promise me this."

"Yes, yes, I do promise. I will, I promise you. Our family is the most important thing there is in life and taking care of them is the most important thing I have to do in this world. I am going to work hard and we are going to make a good life for our children, I swear it."

With a gentleness she did not know was possible under the circumstances, Suzanne continued, "Jonathan is that why you were drinking so much before, did you suspect something?"

Looking down at the ground, Jonathan answered haltingly, "I wondered about it sometimes. It is why I kept saying that if I'd been there, maybe . . . she might not have gone into our bedroom and -- It's all so painful . . . My own mother, how could she?"

Softly, Suzanne answered him, "I know it's hard. I know that you are hurting, we are both hurting, but, Jonathan, I do not think we are ever going to understand why. She was troubled and jealous and it seems somewhat crazy. Yet . . . if we keep dwelling on what she did in the past, in a past that we cannot ever change and, uh . . . if we keep dwelling on what she did, it will all envelop us. We must look forward and not back. We have to pull together, for each other, for the children. We can't let the evil of it win out."

Jonathan stood and looked up at the brilliant blue sky with his head thrown back as though he were trying to absorb the warmth the sun was offering. He looked back down at Suzanne as he answered her, "How did I ever get so lucky to find you? The prettiest girl in the room, in the whole world, the best wife a guy could ever have. I don't know how you can keep right on lovin' me, but I sure am glad that you do."

He reached out for her then and placing her small hand in his, she felt the strength of his grip. As she rose, she grew even more determined to see it through--the valleys, the peaks, and all that comes in between in a lifelong marriage.

Silently they walked hand in hand toward the old family Packard. Suzanne instinctively knew that dealing with this news was going to be the hardest hurdle they had ever faced. Yet, she made up her mind to do it. Maggie Mae's abnormality would not define their family and it would not overcome her heart.

"Jonathan, I don't think we should tell anyone else about this, it would just make it harder, having to talk about it, having other people know what happened, don't you think? She can't be tried for her crimes now that she's dead and buried."

"Honey, I think you're right. Let's just leave people thinking the baby's deaths were a natural occurrence. Let's keep it our secret, a secret between the two of us," Jonathan replied as he stopped to hold her protectively and fiercely.

Suzanne understood that it would be a battle to keep bitterness from filling her heart. She was not certain just how she was going to manage, but she was determined to try. She looked up and saw the foothills of the San Gabriel Mountains in the near distance.

Those were their hills--the hills where they'd walked and laid among the wild sage and lavender, where they'd laughed together and shared their dreams about the future, where they'd picnicked and played with their children. Those mountains were sure, strong, and steadfast. Once more, they enfolded her.

The remembrance of a scripture she had heard the last time she was in church came into Suzanne's mind, "I will lift up mine eyes unto the hills, from whence comes my help."

That was it. Though it would be challenging, her newfound Savior would be beside her as He had been this morning. Her help would come from God. With thankfulness for what she'd found, Suzanne nestled beside Jonathan as they drove away from the graveyard--away from the cold dark abyss and out into the warm autumn sunshine.

Together, they would live in peace. Together they would care for their family. Together, they would make a home that would be a secure harbor, a place of goodness and joy for each other and for each of their children. Suzanne was determined they would make it so! With the help of God, they would make it so.

Watch for the sequel intended for publication in the Fall of 2014